YOU CAN'T HAVE MY PLANET,

BUT TAKE MY BROTHER, PLEASE

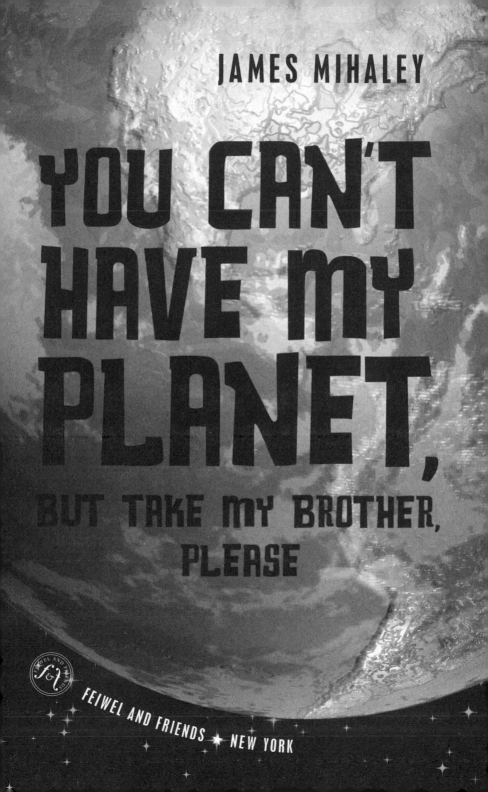

JAMES MIHALEY

YOU CAN'T HAVE MY PLANET,

BUT TAKE MY BROTHER, PLEASE

FEIWEL AND FRIENDS ✦ NEW YORK

A FEIWEL AND FRIENDS BOOK
An Imprint of Macmillan

Printed in the United States of America by
R. R. Donnelley & Sons Company, Harrisonburg, Virginia.
For information, address Feiwel and Friends, 175 Fifth Avenue, New York, N.Y. 10010.

Library of Congress Cataloging-in-Publication Data
Mihaley, James.
You can't have my planet, but take my brother, please / James Mihaley. — 1st ed.
p. cm.
Summary: Thirteen-year-old Giles, a New York City boy who feels invisible next to his talented younger sister and smart older
brother, comes to the rescue when space aliens from an intergalactic realty company arrive and try to evict humans for
polluting the world.
ISBN: 978-0-312-61891-9
[1. Extraterrestrial beings—Fiction.   2. Environmental protection—Fiction.   3. New York (N.Y.)—Fiction.
4. Humorous stories.]   I. Title.   II. Title: You cannot have my planet, but take my brother, please.
PZ7.M59176Yo 2012
[E]—dc23
2011036241

Book design by April Ward

Feiwel and Friends logo designed by Filomena Tuosto

First Edition: 2012

10 9 8 7 6 5 4 3 2 1

mackids.com

FOR MY MOTHER AND FATHER

CHAPTER **ONE**

HI, MY NAME IS GILES.
I'm miserable.

CHAPTER TWO

I'M MISERABLE BECAUSE I just made a complete fool out of myself in front of a cute girl. My sister and I were crouching behind a car in the parking lot at Dale's Diner, playing a make-believe alien game. We were firing lasers at some cyborgs when along comes this cute girl in white shorts whose legs shot up and up like freckled skyscrapers. Her feet lived on the ground floor of those freckled skyscrapers. They were happy living there. I couldn't see how anything wouldn't be happy living there.

I smiled at her. She gave me a "Isn't It Sweet How This Little Boy who Still Wears Diapers Has a Crush on Me" kind of look.

Could you blame her? There I was, holding an imaginary laser gun, making a ridiculous *zoot-zoot* sound. In her eyes I must've looked five, not thirteen like I really was. God, did I feel stupid. I didn't even want to play this alien kiddy game in the first place. It was Nikki's idea. I was only trying to be nice to my little sister, to never turn my back on her like my big brother, Bobby, did to me. As usual, I tried to do the right thing and look where it got me.

Nothing new. Just another lousy day in the life of me, Giles.

Bobby glided into the parking lot on his bike and hopped off. "Come on," he said.

Nikki and I followed him into the diner. When Mom and Dad were away on business, Bobby was second in command behind Grandma.

When Bobby wasn't looking, I grabbed a roll off the table for the raccoons and stashed it in my pocket.

"What do you guys want to drink?" asked the waiter.

"I'll have a nonalcoholic apple martini," said Bobby.

"A what?" asked the waiter.

"A large apple juice," Bobby said.

"A nonalcoholic apple martini," said the waiter. "I like that. I'm going to see if we can put it on the menu."

"I'll have a nonalcoholic apple martini too," said the girl with freckled skyscrapers, who was sitting at the counter, peering over her shoulder at Bobby, gazing into his blue eyes, admiring his long blond hair.

Bobby ignored her. If a girl with freckled skyscrapers ever smiled at me, I would've smiled back. Bobby was always so busy doing practice SAT tests on his iPad he didn't even have time for dating. How stupid is that?

He was such a goodie-goodie. If the goodie-goodies had a kingdom, my brother would be king. He'd be known throughout the land as King Goodie-Goodie.

Gnawing on an onion ring, I couldn't help but notice my lame reflection in the mirror. I was scrawny and pale—a geek without a brain—someone who got decent grades but was certainly no straight A student. Was there a bigger loser on this planet than a geek without a brain?

Dale, the owner of the joint, came over and started talking to us. "When a paper towel falls asleep it's called a napkin. Get it?"

Nikki and I cracked up. Bobby didn't. Goodie-goodies have no sense of humor.

"So I hear you're number one in your class, Bobby," Dale said.

The king nodded.

"Where do you want to go to college?" Dale asked.

"Harvard," Bobby said.

"With those grades you'll be a shoo-in," Dale said, turning to Nikki, pinching her cheek. "And I hear you're quite the violin player."

"I'm not bad," said Nikki.

"Not bad? That's not what your grandma said. She said you're a child prodigy. You'll be going to Juilliard some day."

Nikki blushed.

Dale didn't ask me about all the great stuff I did because there wasn't any. I'm extremely lacking in the great stuff department.

The waiter marched out of the kitchen lugging a big black tray. He handed me my sandwich. I stared at it, belly growling. It was a really big sandwich. I mean a really big sandwich, piled high with roast beef, smoked turkey, salami, Swiss cheese, lettuce and tomato, bean sprouts, mayo, mustard, pickles, hot sauce. Picking it up with both hands, I closed my eyes and opened my mouth wider and wider, stretching my face muscles more than face muscles can possibly stretch. When I took that first big bite, I had to admit, it was hard to taste the meat in the middle. It got drowned out by all the other stuff they loaded on.

Suddenly it occurred to me that my whole life was right there in that sandwich. Just like the meat in the middle, it was hard for me to get noticed in my family. I was the middle child, wedged between a big brother and a younger sister. In the sandwich of my family, I was the flavor that couldn't be tasted.

It ticked me off. I couldn't wait to get out of that darn

diner. As soon as lunch was over I told Bobby I had stuff to do and jumped up from the table.

"Make sure you're back by four," Bobby said. "We're leaving today."

"I know, Bobby. I'm not an idiot."

We lived in New York City. My family had a summer place here in upstate New York, farm country. We'd been here for ten days. Now it was time to head back to the Big Apple.

"If we miss the train because of you, Grandma will go berserk," Bobby said.

"I'll be there," I said. "Now quit bugging me."

I shot out the door.

Whenever I got mad I ran into the forest. It was a great place to hang out when I wanted to be alone. The stillness, the shafts of golden light, the wind sifting through the top branches all teamed up to help calm me down. The beauty of nature sucked the octane out of my fist.

I wandered down a dirt path, the wind on my face and neck and hands. Have you ever been deep inside a gentle breeze? You should try it some time.

Standing still, I closed my eyes and inhaled the fresh scent of cedar and pine. A blue jay rang out in the distance. Another blue jay answered. An ovenbird chirped overhead, then a grouse and a warbler.

My English teacher said I have a gift for writing nature descriptions but she still gave me a B because my grammar sucks. I like writing poetry better because you don't have to worry so much about grammar.

I recited a poem in class once. Big mistake. If you want to get called a sissy just start writing poetry. Wait until the jocks find out. You'll never hear the end of it. Even girls will laugh at you. Take it from me, Giles. Being a poet will never land you a girl with freckled skyscrapers.

All the poetry I write is for me and me only. I whipped out my notebook in the middle of the woods and wrote a short poem called "Summer Vacation."

SUMMER VACATION
We're as tight as can be,
loneliness and me.

I continued on my way through the dark forest. A gust of wind parted the trees. The sun burst through. The gloom began to glow.

I shot up a tree. Despite being a crummy athlete, I had a knack for climbing trees. If tree climbing was an Olympic sport, I'd have a few gold medals by now. I'd have an agent. A bunch of endorsement deals.

Resting on a thick branch way up high, I imagined doing a commercial on TV. "Hi, it's me, Giles. After I've been climbing trees all day, I come home and take a shower with Dial Soap."

I'd be the Tom Brady of tree climbing. All the girls would be after me then. That was my only hope. If tree climbing doesn't become a professional sport then I'll never have a girl-friend.

I climbed down and continued on my way. Pulling the roll out of my pocket, I tore it up into pieces and flung them outside a hole that contained a family of raccoons. Grandma wasn't thrilled that I fed raccoons but I didn't see anything wrong with it. I wasn't stupid enough to try to pet them. I kept on walking, knowing they wouldn't come out until I was long gone.

Marching past a giant oak, I glanced up at the remnants of a tree fort Bobby and I built two years ago. I stared at it like you'd stare at a pyramid from a lost civilization, back when life was good, back when Bobby and I hung out together all the time. Before he decided that he was too old to play with me anymore.

We carefully selected this tree because the canopy provided perfect camouflage and was undetectable by alien warlords ransacking Earth. After six hours of nailing boards into branches, we christened our fort with a bottle of Gatorade. Then we drilled spy holes all around the floor and walls in order to engage in alien surveillance and bird-watching.

We were so thrilled with our fort we formed our own architecture firm, specializing in tree houses. We had business cards printed up and passed them out to kids at Dale's Diner.

I picked up a rock and threw it at the tree house. The architecture firm went out of business when Bobby hit ninth grade and his grades started counting for college. I couldn't get Bobby's betrayal out of my mind.

Sweat dripped down my forehead. It was the middle of a heat wave. It was the middle of July. The middle is a universe unto its own. It was my universe. And it was a pretty lousy one. I was tired of it, tired of being stuck in the middle of my family. I couldn't wait to show everyone that I wasn't a big nobody, that I added a unique spicy flavor to the double-decker sandwich of this world.

Standing in the middle of the forest, I prayed for something really cool to happen. What I longed for was a quest, an adventure, something grand and daring that would show the world just how brave and important I was. Something that would prove once and for all that I was just as good as Bobby.

I prayed so hard, rocking back and forth from side to

side, gritting my teeth, my cheeks all puffed out, a vein in my forehead throbbing . . . I guess the universe decided to answer my prayer before my brain exploded.

Suddenly the wind picked up, lashing the trees. The hot gusts got stronger and stronger until the whole forest shook violently. I had to dodge the falling branches. It was a tornado. Unlike any tornado I'd ever seen on TV, this one gave off a blinding light. Even stranger, this tornado wasn't funnel shaped. This tornado was round. This tornado wasn't a tornado, it was a—oh my God, it couldn't be—this tornado was a spaceship.

CHAPTER **THREE**

ON THE SIDE of the spaceship, in big black letters, it read, INTER-
GALACTIC REALTY. A picture of an alien was painted on the
hatch. His skin was zebra striped but the stripes were red and
orange, not black and white. Below the picture it read: JERRY,
IF I CAN'T SELL IT, NO ONE CAN!

I shot up the tree into the fort. Whipping out my cell
phone, I called 911 but it didn't work. They must've jammed
the signal. Aliens can do that.

I peeked through a spy hole. Down below, the hatch
opened and the Jerry guy emerged. His long blond dreadlocks jutted out of his head like cornstalks, pointing straight
up instead of straight down. He was decked out in a silver
suit that had more glitter on it than a sixteen-year-old girl at
a makeup party. He kept admiring his portrait on the side of
the spaceship. This alien was really into himself.

He planted a sign in the ground: OPEN HOUSE FROM 1 TO 4!

I glanced at my watch, 12:59. At precisely one p.m. another spaceship landed.

Two elderly aliens came shuffling out, a male and a female, both wearing gold crowns and long velvet robes. There
was something classy about them, even though they both had
dark purple skin and beady eyes that glowed.

The queen, or at least I assumed she was a queen, was reading something Jerry gave her. Silently, stealthily, I grabbed a plastic telescope out of the battle-supply kit Bobby and I kept stored in the tree fort, pressed it up against my right eye and zeroed in on the thing she was reading.

It was a brochure like the kind your parents might have if they were planning to buy a house. A brochure like that would list the number of bathrooms the house contained. It would show fancy pictures of the living room, the dining room, the pool in the backyard. It would list the square footage of the house and the number of fireplaces.

But the brochure the queen held in her purple hand was for someone who was interested in purchasing an entire planet. It listed the circumference of Earth, 24,901 miles, the diameter, 7926 miles. It described the seven continents and the four major oceans. It was filled with dazzling photographs of the Great Barrier Reef, the Grand Canyon, the Great Wall of China.

Earth was for sale? Heck no! Not if I had anything to say about it.

The queen flipped the page. She stared at a photo of Egypt. She turned to the king. "Oh, Leonard, aren't they cute?"

"What are they?" said the king.

"They're called pyramids, King Zoodle," Jerry replied. "They're used to store the dead. Of course, you can use them to store anything."

"Garden equipment?" asked King Zoodle.

"Absolutely," Jerry said. "Although you won't be doing much gardening in the desert." He bobbed his head in harmony with the swaying trees and smiled at the queen. "But you'll be doing plenty right here, Queen Mooby. This is some of the most fertile soil in the entire universe. Because of all the deforestation on your planet, I thought you'd want to see it before the pyramids."

"Absolutely," said Queen Mooby.

They came to steal our crops. Suddenly I was convinced of that. They were conspiring to sneak off with all the corn and soybeans. They were here to steal everything edible. I tried to warn my brother with a text message but it didn't go through. The signal was still jammed.

Jerry led the royal couple down the dirt path, heading directly toward the tree fort. Why couldn't they go the other way?

"Are you sure there aren't any humans around?" the queen said nervously.

"Absolutely," insisted Jerry. "They're all at the mall."

They were directly below me.

"As you can see," Jerry said, "I don't waste my time on second-rate properties. I only get the prime listings. I'm the top dog. The king of Intergalactic Realty." He leaned forward, flirting with the queen. "I'm royalty, baby."

Queen Mooby blushed.

I was trying to figure out how to text NASA when I saw the snake. It crawled out from inside a Burger King bag on the other end of the tree fort and stared at me. Just my luck. I was trapped in a tree house with a big black snake. I waved my fist in the air but the snake didn't back away. Aliens on the outside, a snake on the inside. Let me tell you. I just love summer vacation.

The snake coiled and hissed.

I felt like yelling, "Hey, I built this tree fort, you lousy serpent. You get out."

But I got the feeling the snake was in no mood to listen. I

was so crazed, so delirious, I could almost hear the snake say, "Listen, bozo, if you don't get out of my master bedroom in five seconds, I'm going to bite you a couple of hundred times. You're better off dealing with the aliens than with me."

The snake had a point there.

Before I could decide what to do the big black snake turned into a little bitty worm. That did not make a whole lot of sense to me. I slowly turned around. That Jerry creature lurked by the entrance to the fort, aiming what must've been a shrinking gadget at the snake. I mean the worm.

"Thanks," I said in a total daze. "You saved my life."

"Don't mention it," Jerry said. "What name do you go by, Earthling?"

"Giles."

"Come on down, Giles. I'll introduce you to everyone."

I climbed down and followed him cautiously over by the royal couple.

"Oh no!" shrieked the queen. "It's a . . . human."

The king stared at me in stunned disbelief. "Why aren't you at the mall?"

"I hate malls."

"Just our luck," muttered the king.

"Relax," Jerry said. "Giles is our friend."

Friend? Not if they were trying to take over the planet or steal our crops, I wasn't. I love corn on the cob. I wasn't about to let aliens take it. But they could definitely have the Brussels sprouts. I'd help them load up the mothership.

"Is it true?" asked King Zoodle. "Do you come in peace?"

"I sure do," I said, not entirely believing that.

"Did you hear that? He comes in peace." The queen

breathed a sigh of relief. She studied me curiously. "So you humans aren't bloodthirsty after all?"

"No way," I said.

"It just goes to show that you can't trust stereotypes," she said.

We hung out for half an hour. I couldn't believe how nice they were. If you ever get a chance to hang out with aliens I highly recommend it. We've been brainwashed to believe they're evil. Well, let me fill you in on something. The same guy who said aliens are evil probably thinks chocolate chip cookie dough sucks. That gives you an idea of his IQ.

"Do you guys need a place to live?" I asked.

The king sighed wearily. "That's all I'm looking for. A place where my wife and I can live in peace and not be bothered."

That didn't sound evil and treacherous. It sounded kind of sad.

"My family has a summer home on the other side of the woods," I told them. "It'll be empty all winter. You can live there."

"Do you really think so?" Queen Mooby said, squeezing my hand.

"Absolutely," I said.

They didn't need to launch an attack. I'm sure my parents would give it to them to avoid an all out invasion.

I was an ambassador, negotiating a peace treaty between us and extraterrestrials. Do they give out the Nobel Peace Prize to kids? If not, then they need to change the rules.

"That certainly is very kind of you," said the queen.

"I'm happy to do it," I said.

"Where are your parents?" asked Jerry.

"Malaysia. My mom and dad are venture capitalists. That's another name for a big-time investor. They have their own company. Nimmer and Nimmer. They get written up in *The Wall Street Journal* all the time."

"How long will they be gone?" Jerry asked.

"Three more weeks," I said.

Jerry leaned over and whispered something to the king.

"Hey, Jerry," I said. "Why weren't you scared of me like the king and queen were?"

"I've interacted with humans before. I sold a condo on Mars to an astronaut who wanted to get away from his wife. Boy, did I rip him off." He patted me on the head. "Just kidding."

Another spaceship came zooming down to join the party, darting all around, searching for a place to land. With two spaceships already in the clearing, there wasn't any room to park a third one. It hovered directly above us, making a deafening roar, its engine spewing hot air in our faces.

An alien popped his green head out of the hatch, fixed three eyes on the king and yelled, "Where do you want me to park this thing?"

"How am I supposed to know?" said the king, deeply offended. He straightened his crown. "Do I look like a valet to you?"

"If you're not a valet, then who is?"

"They don't have valet parking," said the king, frowning at Jerry.

I nudged Jerry and whispered excitedly, "Hey, Jerry, I'll park his spaceship for him."

Jerry smiled up at the alien. "Of course we have valet parking." He pointed proudly at me. "This is a first-class operation."

The alien eyed me suspiciously. He didn't seem scared of me, just extremely unimpressed. "Are sure you he knows how to drive?"

"Are you kidding me?" Jerry said. "Do you know how many video games this boy has played? He knows that star cruiser like the back of his hand. Don't you, Giles?"

"Um . . . of course I do. I could drive that thing blind-folded."

When you get a chance to drive a spaceship you don't pass it up.

The green guy peering down at us shut off the engine on his spaceship. Somehow it remained silently suspended in mid-air. A ramp slid out of its silver belly and he came trotting down, wearing special sunglasses for three eyes. "OK, kid," he said, tossing me a gold key. "Don't get any scratches on it."

I ran up the ramp and closed the hatch before he could change his mind. There I was, inside a spaceship. I stood there for a minute, paralyzed by the coolness of intergalactic technology. The gold key in my hand pulsed with light. I wondered why he gave it to me because there was no ignition to stick it in. There were at least one hundred buttons on the console. Not one of them read: START ENGINE. I was tempted to just start pressing buttons but I didn't want to slam the thing in reverse by mistake and knock down a bunch of beautiful old pine trees. What if I accidentally vaporized a flock of swallows?

Just as I was about to give up and go back outside I heard a voice. Well, I didn't actually hear it. It was a voice in my head, a soundless whisper in the center of my brain.

Welcome, Earthling. This is 2012 Star Cruiser. I am equipped with thought-activation technology. Just think where you want to go and I will take you there.

Are you talking to me?

Yes, Earthling. I'm talking to you.

Wait, hold on a second. Are you saying that all I have to do is think about a place and you'll park this baby over there?

That is an accurate statement, Earthling.

(Hey, reader, I'm not using quotation marks here because the computer and I weren't actually talking out loud. No words came out of my mouth. Don't start getting all confused. It's very simple. When you read what sounds like dialogue but there are no quotation marks, then you know I'm talking to the spaceship. I know you can handle that, regardless of what grade you got in English last semester.)

(Come on, dude. Don't start freaking out. Here's another way to look at it. The spaceship and I played a bizarre game of catch. It tossed a thought into my head. I Frisbeed a thought back.)

OK, spaceship. Here's what I want you to do. There's another clearing over behind those oak trees. Go park over there.

As you wish, Earthling.

It flew over there and landed.

Is there anything else I can do for you, Earthling?

I kicked back in the driver's seat, marveling at the gauges on the instrument panel, each one blinking and flickering.

Does this thing have a HowmanytimeshaveIscratched mybutt-ometer?

No, Earthling. I am not equipped with a Howmanytimes-haveIscratchedmybutt-ometer.

Then how am I supposed to keep track of how many times I scratched my butt?

I have no idea, Earthling.

Just kidding.

Your species has an odd sense of humor.

I'm a New Yorker.

Well, that explains it.

Do you have a stereo?

Yes, I do.

Crank that sucker!

All of a sudden the music kicked in. It was louder than a rock concert. It *was* a rock concert. A hologram of an alien punk band flashed upon the dashboard. The lead singer had three heads. Two of them had Mohawks. The third head, which had a puffy purple afro, sang lead vocals while the other two heads sang backup.

The lead guitarist was a cyborg. The bongos had arms and hands and played themselves.

I listened to three songs then ran back over by Jerry and the others.

"It's about time," Jerry said. "You've got two other star cruisers to park."

I didn't know what they were all doing here but in the excitement it didn't seem to matter.

The next spaceship I climbed inside was older and more beat up than the first one I parked. Loose wires dangled from the dashboard. The cushion on the pilot's seat had a rip in it. It scattered bits of fluff in the air when I plopped down on it.

How's it going, spaceship?

The spaceship didn't answer.

There's a cave on the other side of that stream up ahead. Go park over there.

The star cruiser didn't budge.

I said, go park over by the cave.

It didn't move. It didn't say anything to me either. No soundless whisper rang out in the center of my brain.

Maybe the older model spaceships didn't have thought-activation technology. Like a 1962 Chevy wouldn't have a DVD player in the backseat.

That meant I had to drive this thing with my own two hands. But how?

Before I could press a button, something attacked me. It was slimy. It was howling. It was hurtling through the air. It knocked me to the ground, pinned me to the floor. I kicked and screamed but couldn't fight it off.

In the middle of my panic, something occurred to me. I wasn't in any pain. How can you not be in any pain if something is eating your face? I guess it wasn't chomping on my cheeks or gnawing on my nose. Instead it was . . . it was licking me! I was getting licked by an alien.

This thing, whatever it was, liked me a lot. It was an alien creature with long whiskers and a cute wet black face that reminded me of a seal. Its body was cyborgish, made out of metal in a squat shape like an armadillo. If I had to give it a name I'd call it a sealadillo.

Grabbing a stick off the floor, the creature dropped it in my lap and backed up excitedly, waiting for me to throw it, just like a dog would. It had a collar around its neck. This thing was someone's pet.

I tossed the stick to the other side of the spaceship. The creature darted after it. On its way back, it dropped the stick and aimed its snout at a can of orange sardine-like things on a table. Sealadillo treats!

I dangled a sardine in the air. "I'll give you a treat if you fly this thing over by the cave."

He hopped in the copilot's seat and jabbed some buttons with his snout.

We took off.

Don't ever let anyone tell you sealadillos are stupid. They're highly intelligent creatures. As soon as we landed, I tossed him the sardine. He gulped it down and bounded into my arms, tickling me with his whiskers. I heard Jerry calling my name in the distance. I gave the sealadillo a big hug and took off.

The third star cruiser I parked was much smaller, about the size of an SUV. As soon as I climbed in, I heard someone say, in a real voice—not just a thought in my brain, but an actual grunting voice—

"Make sure you don't dent the fender."

I glanced around uneasily. "Who said that?"

"I did."

I looked down. It was the key chain in my hand, a shrunken head key chain. It was alive, staring up at me. I dropped it and screamed.

"That hurts," it said, bouncing on the floor.

I took a deep breath and picked it up. "Sorry about that."

"Don't worry about it."

Having a normal conversation with a key chain isn't easy. I couldn't think of anything to say.

"How do you like being a key chain?" I finally blurted.

"It sucks. I mean having a shrunken head wasn't exactly a goal of mine. When I was a kid, I didn't go around saying when I grow up I want to be a key chain. How do you think my parents feel? They don't exactly brag about it. Oh, your son's a doctor? Well, my son's a key chain."

"Who turned you into a key chain?" I said.

"A wizard on Jupiter. He didn't want me dating his daughter." He lowered his voice. "You're in big trouble, Earthling. I mean really big trouble."

"Hey, at least I'm not a key chain."

The shrunken head started crying.

"I'm sorry," I said. "I didn't mean that."

I dug into my pocket and gave him half a Kleenex. A shrunken head doesn't need a whole Kleenex. You're wasting paper and that's environmentally irresponsible.

"What do you mean I'm in trouble?" I said.

"The king and queen aren't just looking for a home for themselves," said the shrunken head. "They're looking for a home for their entire population. We're talking fifty million purple creatures walking around on Earth."

"A mass invasion," I gasped.

I couldn't believe I actually thought of them as my purple buddies.

"When are they going to attack?" I asked.

"There won't be an attack. They don't need to. You humans are getting kicked off the planet. One morning you'll wake up and you'll all be gone."

"What do you mean?" I said.

"They'll beam you off the planet while you're fast asleep. You won't even know what hit you."

"Can they do that?"

"You're darn right they can. I'm not talking about the king and queen either. There are higher-ups involved."

"Higher than a king and queen?" I said.

"A lot higher. This thing goes all the way to the top."

"Where will they send us?"

"To Desoleen," he said.

"Desoleen? What's that?"

"It's a wasteland. I'd rather be a key chain than get sent there."

"But why?" I asked. "What did we do?"

"They say you don't take care of the planet. They say you're lousy tenants. So they're evicting you."

"We can't get evicted," I said. "We own our apartment in Manhattan. We don't rent."

"Don't you get it? This isn't about your family. This is about your species. Your entire species is about to get evicted from planet Earth."

"No way. You can't evict six billion people."

"That's what you think," said the shrunken head.

"It doesn't make sense," I said. "If they're out to get me, then why did that Jerry guy save me from a snake?"

"It wasn't a real snake. He planted it there so he could gain your trust. It's all a put-on. He's trying to sell Earth so he can get rich."

I gritted my teeth. "That weasel. He doesn't know who he's dealing with!"

I left the key chain in the spaceship and snuck back over by Jerry, who was talking to the king and queen. I ducked behind a tree, spying on their conversation.

"I say we grab Earth before someone else does," said Queen Mooby.

"Your wife is a very intelligent woman, King Zoodle," said Jerry.

"But Earth only has one moon," the king complained.

"So?" said Jerry.

"There's nothing I hate more than looking up at the sky and seeing one lousy moon," moaned the king.

Although I remained silent, I felt like yelling, "Hey, dude, don't go dissing the moon. It's perfect."

As a poet, I felt obligated to defend the moon. We poets worship it.

"If you can't deal with one moon, then what are we going to do?" asked the queen.

"Why do we have to move?" asked the king. "Why can't we just stay where we are?"

"Well, Your Excellency," said Jerry, "I guess it has something to do with the fact that you've run out of water on your planet and are about to run out of oxygen and your subjects are about to storm the palace and drag you through the streets."

"Fine," said King Zoodle. "We'll take it."

"Excellent." Jerry whipped out a contract and handed the king a pen. "Sign here."

King Mooby signed.

Jerry beckoned the green alien with three eyes and the others who were wandering around the forest, taking samples of the soil and measuring the width of the trees.

"We have a buyer," Jerry told them.

"Hey," hissed the three-eyed creature, "I didn't even get a chance to make an offer."

"Neither did I," howled another alien.

"That's right," Jerry said. "I've run credit checks on all of you. The king is the only one who can actually afford this place."

I crawled out of the bush. "What's going on?"

Jerry hid the contract behind his back. "Nothing."

"Nothing at all," said the king.

"Don't you think it's time you told him?" said the queen.

"Told me what?" I said. "That we're getting evicted?"

At first Jerry was shocked that I knew. Then he seemed delighted. "That's right. You humans are getting evicted. They're sending you to Desoleen. And there's nothing you can do about it."

"Oh yeah," I said. "Wait till the marines find out. They've got smart bombs."

"What's a smart bomb?" asked the three-eyed alien.

"A smart bomb can fly across the Atlantic in a minute and a half, wipe out four different targets, then fly back across the ocean, pick up a pepperoni pizza, drop it off at your house and wipe out four more targets. How does that sound?"

"Sounds wonderful," Jerry said, strutting back and forth. "Where can I get one?"

"At the Pentagon," I said.

"Do they have a drive-thru?" Jerry asked.

"Doesn't everyone?" said King Zoodle, chuckling.

They all burst out laughing, except Queen Mooby.

She gently put her hand on my shoulder. "I feel sorry for the child. No one deserves to be sent to Desoleen."

"We're not going anywhere," I said. "You can't do this to the human race. There are billions of us."

"I'm afraid you don't have a choice," said the queen.

"She's right," said Jerry. "Here. See for yourself." Reaching into his jacket, he handed me an ancient scroll. "Here's a copy of the lease. You have violated the agreement. Now you must suffer the penalty."

They plunged into the woods to go find their spaceships.

"Come on, King Zoodle," Jerry murmured from the shadows. "Let's get out of here. The humans will be gone in a couple of days. Then you can move in."

I unrolled the scroll and stared at it, dumbfounded. It was covered with symbols that were indecipherable. There were two signatures at the bottom: Adam and Eve.

Holding the gold parchment in my hands, I watched the spaceships rise up, one by one, and disappear into the sky.

CHAPTER FOUR

GRANDMA STOOD ON THE EDGE of the driveway, calling frantically, "Giles! Giles!"

"Here I am, Grandma." I ran into her arms.

Stressing out Grandma was not something I wanted to do.

She pressed me to her chest. "I've been searching all over for you."

"Don't worry, Grandma," I said. "I'll go pack right now. We won't miss the train."

"Don't forget to put on a sweater."

"But, Grandma," I said. "It's ninety degrees out."

"Not on the train it isn't. You'll catch pneumonia in that air-conditioning."

Should I tell her about the aliens? No, it might give her a heart attack. She was already in rough shape. She looked pale, thin and sickly. She started wasting away six months ago, right after Grandpa died. They were married fifty-three years.

Grandma lost her soul mate. When you lose your soul mate, life is bad enough. The last thing you need to hear about is aliens.

"I'll put on a really thick sweater, Grandma," I said, sprinting up the driveway.

I stopped, panting, sweating, trying to formulate a strategy. An alien takeover. This crisis was too big for the police or the fire department. I had to go directly to the president. No problem. I'll just call the Oval Office and tell his secretary it's me, Giles. I'm sure she'll put me right through. Even if he's in a meeting with a prime minister, she'll interrupt it because I'm a top priority.

"Excuse me, Mr. President," she'll say, "I've got Giles on the line."

Yeah, right. The chances of me getting through to the president were one in a trillion.

Nikki was playing the violin on our front porch, a normal thing to do, except this time she was standing on her pink suitcase.

"Why are you standing on your suitcase?" I asked.

"I'm experiencing life at a different altitude," she said.

Nikki was only six. A six-year-old girl should not be told that aliens are trying to get us kicked off Earth. Even a six-year-old who uses big words like *altitude*.

I raced inside and dashed upstairs. Bobby was in his bedroom packing for our trip back home to Manhattan.

I shut the door, locked it. I was so excited I could barely get the words out. "Bobby, Bobby, I . . . I had an alien encounter."

"Sure you did," he said, carefully packing his debate team trophy.

"I'm serious. In the woods. They were . . . they were real aliens."

"Real aliens, huh? What kind of aliens?"

"Well, there was a realtor."

"An alien realtor?" He snickered.

"Bobby, I'm serious. This isn't make-believe. I hid in the tree fort."

"Does the alien realtor want to sell our tree fort?"

"No," I said.

"Why not?"

"He wants to sell Earth instead."

"You mean the whole planet?"

"The whole planet." I grabbed him by the arm. "We're getting evicted, Bobby. Our entire species. Humankind is getting kicked off the planet."

Bobby burst out laughing and patted me on the head. "Then you'd better protect us, little guy."

I clenched my fist. I hated it when he called me little guy. He was only two inches taller and two years, two days and four hours older than me.

I was tempted to whip out the lease Jerry gave me but decided against it. What was the point? Bobby wouldn't think it was real anyway. Maybe it wasn't. Maybe it never happened. Maybe I fell asleep in the woods and dreamed the whole thing. After all, if aliens came down to Earth, they wouldn't waste their time talking to me. They'd go talk to the guy who invented Krispy Kreme donuts.

I decided that it was all in my head and vowed never to think about it again for the rest of my life or in any future life if there was such a thing as reincarnation; but I didn't think there was because I'm not some fool who believes in reincarnation or aliens.

I slunk into my bedroom and tossed dirty clothes into a tattered suitcase. I pulled the lease out of my pocket and unrolled it. If everything was a figment of my imagination then what was this ancient document? It was written in symbols. There were circles looped together, three or four to a bunch. There were dozens of circles piled on top of each other in heaps. A few circles stood by themselves. Those circles all had x's in the middle. There were upside-down triangles, octagons with dots inside. Everything was written in black ink except for some vertical bars, which were bright red. None of it made any sense to me. The only thing I could comprehend were the two signatures at the bottom. That was definitely an ADAM and that was definitely an EVE.

A strange buzzing sound rang in my ear. I glanced over my shoulder. A hummingbird hovered right next to my head, its tiny emerald wings beating feverishly. Last summer I attached a hummingbird feeder outside my window, so I usually get hummingbirds out there, but this was the first time one actually flew into my bedroom. Hummingbirds never come this close to humans.

It was only inches away. I could've sworn it was reading the lease. If a hummingbird is going to fly into your room and read an ancient scroll, that means the scroll has to be real. If I was reading about yetis in the *National Enquirer*, the hummingbird wouldn't waste its time.

It darted out the window, flew over to a blue jay on a swaying branch and twittered something. It was telling the blue jay about the lease! I knew this with a certainty I couldn't explain. It was all real. I wasn't losing my mind. I did have an alien encounter. For a split second I wasn't scared of being evicted. I wasn't concerned about it at all. I was thrilled and honored and overjoyed that the first kid in the history of the world ever to have contact with aliens was me, Giles. The first kid ever to valet park UFOs was me, Giles. The first kid ever to get licked by a sealadillo was, that's right, me, Giles. I think I'll say it again for good luck. Me, Giles.

You're probably wondering why you're reading a book that has the writer always saying "me, Giles." Well, don't worry. Lots of really cool stuff happens in the following chapters that will blow your mind. And the cool thing that was happening to me at this particular moment was that for once in my life I felt more important than Bobby.

"Come on, everyone!" Grandma yelled from downstairs. "It's time to leave!"

"New York City here we come!" Nikki shouted.

I got a minute alone with Grandma at the station. Nikki and Bobby were off getting candy for the train ride.

"Grandma, can we go visit the White House?" I said.

"Certainly," she said.

"Right now?" I said.

She gave me a long look. "Right now, Giles?"

"Yes. We can change our train tickets from Manhattan to Washington D.C."

I pictured myself on a tour of the White House, breaking away from the tour group, sneaking past secret service agents into the Oval Office.

"Giles," Grandma said, "a trip like that has to be planned out months in advance. We'd have to book hotel reservations."

"But, Grandma, I want to go right now. You don't understand. This is very important."

"Giles, it's out of the question. Nikki has violin lessons this week. Bobby has an SAT seminar to attend."

"Who cares about a stupid SAT seminar?" I said.

Bobby twisted my arm. "What was that?"

"Knock it off, you two," Grandma said. "It's time to board the train."

Bobby let me go, smirking. "Six billion people getting evicted. That's good, Giles. That's really good."

For a moment, and this was highly unusual, I actually

enjoyed the fact that my brother was teasing me. I deserved to get taunted. It was ridiculous to think an entire species could get evicted.

I took my seat on the train, trying with all my might to believe that the key chain was messing with my head. He was a liar. That must've been why he got his head shrunk in the first place. He probably lied to the wizard and the wizard didn't appreciate it.

Shrunken heads are not known for their honesty.

I imagined that the president and I were having a serious conversation:

"Who told you we we're getting evicted, Giles?"

"A shrunken head."

"A shrunken head told you we're getting evicted?"

"That's right, Mr. President."

The president and all his generals burst out laughing. I could hear them cackling over the roar of the train.

But it wasn't just the shrunken head. Jerry said we were getting evicted too. So did the king and queen. They said we were getting kicked off the planet. But what if it was all a hoax, a great big scam? Jerry could've planted the shrunken head just like he planted the snake, hoping that if he got us scared enough we might evacuate Earth on our own.

Or what if none of this was happening at all? What if . . . what if I was hallucinating because of my cell phone? People were always saying cell phones were bad for you. The radiation zapped my brain cells and now I was seeing things.

But the lease seemed so real.

I didn't know what to do or who to tell or where to start but at least my life wasn't boring anymore. That was a major victory.

Bobby eyed me suspiciously. "What are you smiling about?"

"Never mind," I said, reaching into my pocket, gently running my fingers over the scroll.

Oh, how my brother would want it. Just the lease alone could get him into Harvard. All he'd have to do is saunter into the admissions department waving the gold parchment in the air. "Here, take a look at this. Now let me into Harvard."

But I vowed never to show it to him.

Nikki leaped from her seat across the aisle into Grandma's lap. "Grandma, did you know that when hippos are dishonest it's called hippo-pocrisy?"

"Yeah," I said, "and a dishonest rapper is a hip-hop-acrite."

"You children are so clever," Grandma said. "I have the cleverest RFLs in New York City."

Grandma called us grandkids her RFLs, her "reasons for living."

The train wound through rolling hills. A tractor glinted in the distance, dragging some dead branches. It rumbled down a dirt road. Overhead, three purple clouds floated in the same direction, as if they were tied to the tractor. The farmer was hauling purple clouds, pruning the summer sky, leaving it bright and blue and vast. This planet was breathtaking. No wonder King Zoodle wanted it.

I kept running my fingers over the ancient scroll.

As usual, Bobby tried to act like the star of the family. "Guess what?" he said. "I'm writing a book."

"So am I," Nikki said.

Bobby frowned at her. "What's your book called, Nikki?"

"*How to Eat a Meatball*," she said.

Grandma burst out laughing. "That's the best title I've ever heard."

"It's about ice cream," Nikki said.

Bobby rolled his eyes. "You're writing a book about ice cream called *How to Eat a Meatball*?"

"It's going to be a best-seller," Grandma said.

"I bet," Bobby said. "My book is called *How to Get Your Homework Done*."

"I like *How to Eat a Meatball* better," I said.

"You would," Bobby muttered.

Normally a remark like that would've annoyed me but today it bounced right off. The most important document in the history of the world was rolled up in my right pocket. That can work wonders on a person's ego.

(Hey, reader, can you believe I took a shot at my brother in my book title? Wait till he finds out. He'll be so mad!)

An hour later, the train pulled into Grand Central Station. A black limo was waiting to pick us up. Did I tell you my parents were loaded? The driver took our bags and we hopped inside. The limo crawled uptown through heavy traffic.

Bobby kept on rambling about his stupid book. "You know how many kids have trouble getting their homework done?" he said, pointing at you know who.

"Don't look at me," I blurted. "I do my homework." It was true. The problem was, I still didn't get straight As. No matter how hard I studied I would never be as smart as Bobby. But who cared? When you hold the fate of humankind in your right pocket no one cares what you got on your last algebra test.

"Having poor study habits is a worldwide epidemic," Bobby declared.

"And you're just the one to solve the problem," Grandma said, patting Bobby on the knee.

"Someone needs to solve the problem of all that trash," I said, staring sadly out the window.

When you go away to the country and come back, you realize just how filthy New York City is. Don't get me wrong. I love New York. It's the coolest, greatest, grandest, hippest, holiest metropolis in the world. But it's filthy. And it stinks, especially in the summer. Garbage and graffiti are everywhere. Could something like that cause an entire species to get thrown off a planet?

"Hey, Grandma," Nikki said, "did you know that trash talking actually means trash talking?"

"No, it doesn't," Bobby said. "Trash talking is a term used in sports when one player taunts another."

"That's what you think," Nikki said.

"What is the trash saying, Nikki?" Grandma asked.

Nikki peered out at the grimy sidewalk. "That hot dog wrapper just said, 'I'm so happy people litter.'"

Nikki pulled out a block of chocolate and began chomping on it. She had the biggest sweet tooth in New York City. Because of that, Nikki was a little chubby but that only added to her little kid cuteness. If aliens ever tried to hurt my little sister, boy, would they be sorry. I'd wipe out every single one of them. I was not someone you wanted to mess with. Just ask the video game monsters. If there was such a thing as a video game monster graveyard, it was a heckuva lot bigger because of me, Giles. I was a video game sharpshooter. No one was better at killing video game monsters than I was.

Nikki tossed me the block of chocolate. I broke off a piece and handed it to Grandma. "Here, Grandma. Have something to eat."

"I'm not hungry, Giles."

"But, Grandma, you need to eat."

"I'll be fine," she said.

I wasn't so sure about that. Grandma had lost twenty

pounds since Grandpa died. She was skinny to begin with. Now she looked emaciated.

I shoved the chocolate into her lap. "Please, Grandma."

"OK, Giles," she said, nibbling on it. "Now let's be quiet so your brother can read. Charles Dickens requires great concentration."

"Finally someone in this family has a rational thing to say," Bobby said, reading *A Tale of Two Cities*. He glanced up at me and cringed. "Giles, there's a bee on your leg."

"So?" I just let it sit there. It wasn't bothering anybody.

"What do you mean so?" Bobby said, getting ready to nail it with his book.

Before he could harm it, I rolled down the window and let it fly away. It sailed across Fifty-seventh Street into Central Park.

The limo driver eyed me in the rearview mirror like I was crazy. I didn't care. I don't kill anything. Not even ants.

We pulled up at a red light. A man crossed the street with a Great Dane. It stopped and sniffed a poodle. People say nature doesn't exist in cities. If that's true, then what are dogs and cats and squirrels and bees and butterflies? And what about pigeons? I love the way they sail over traffic jams. It's like they're saying, "Ha-ha, we can glide over gridlock and you can't."

I have a telescope in my bedroom. I don't use it to snoop on neighbors. I use it for bird-watching. I keep it aimed at Central Park. I've identified forty-nine different kinds of birds.

What if my days as a bird-watcher were about to come to an end? What if I woke up tomorrow morning on a wasteland? What if they didn't have a single bird on Desoleen? What if I was taken from Earth without ever having seen a satin bowerbird or a jabiru or a kookaburra or a rainbow lorikeet? Those birds were native to Australia. Ever since I was five and wore kangaroo pajamas, my great goal in life has been to visit Australia. Would I be evicted from this planet before I had a chance to explore the Land Down Under?

Would I ever get to kiss a girl? That was another great goal of mine. I got the distinct impression from the shrunken head that there wasn't a lot of kissing taking place on Desoleen.

The limo pulled up outside our building on Central Park West.

"Home at last," Grandma said.

The doorman grabbed our bags. We took the elevator up thirty floors to the penthouse.

I helped Grandma to her room. I made her a cup of chamomile tea in the kitchen and brought it to her. She was staring at a photograph of Grandpa on the wall. I let her kiss me on the cheek, then I dashed back into the kitchen. I grabbed a box of glazed donuts and ran into my room. I bolted the door, sat down at my desk and gorged on a mouthwatering donut. I wiped my hands on my shirt. I wiped them on my socks. Never before have I made such a big deal out of cleaning my hands. Hand cleaning is not a major priority for me but this time I made sure every drop of powdered sugar was off my fingers. When they were finally immaculate, I pulled out the lease, spread it across my desk and beheld the ancient document.

Trying in vain to read the confusing symbols, I had the odd sensation that someone was watching me. I slowly turned around. It was an alien. My heart bounced inside my chest on a trampoline of terror. It was here to assassinate me. I knew too much. I may not have understood the lease but I knew about the eviction. That meant I had to die.

CHAPTER FIVE

I CONSIDERED LUNGING for the baseball bat in my closet but it was
too far away, so I did the next best thing. I grabbed the box
of donuts. "Want a donut?" I asked, the box trembling in my
hand.

"No, thank you," said the alien.

"They're really good. I mean they're a lot better when
they're warm. And they've come right off the conveyor belt.
And the frosting is all gooey 'cuz they just went underneath
the waterfall of glaze. That's what they call it. 'The waterfall
of glaze,'" I babbled.

The alien stared at me.

"If I were a donut I think it would be cool to pass underneath the waterfall of glaze." I flashed a frightened smile. "Of
course I'm not a donut. Donuts are things you eat. You don't
eat me." I gulped. "Do you?"

"No, of course not." The alien smiled. "Please allow me
to introduce myself. My name is Tula."

Now that I knew I wasn't going to be munched on, my
brain started functioning again. It was a girl, an alien girl.
She had human features but her face was pale blue like a clear
sky and just as bright. She was luminous. Her puffy blond
cloud-shaped hair reminded me of golden cotton candy. She

was a sky creature, a sky chick but without feathers or a beak or any other bird-like quality. Even if she couldn't fly, she looked like she belonged in midair. I half expected to see a miniature sun peek out from inside her cloudy hairdo.

She wore a long gold skirt and matching suit coat, very adult-like, carrying a tan briefcase. She seemed all business, despite her skyness.

The buttons on her jacket glowed. They were huge and round and moon-like, dotted with tiny craters.

"What's up with those buttons?" I said.

"Nothing," she replied.

"Nothing?" I said. "That's a good one. I saw a shrunken head this afternoon. Those are shrunken planets, aren't they?"

"No, they're just buttons."

"What can they do?"

"I can button my coat with them."

"What else can they do? Can they deflect ray guns? I mean if someone fires a laser at you will it bounce off your buttons?"

"No. They don't have any force-field capability."

"Can they talk?"

"No, they're just buttons. Just large round buttons. Do you understand?"

"Yes," I said, embarrassed, "they're just buttons."

I think she was a little irritated. I have a way of annoying people. I can't help it.

"I've been appointed by the court to provide legal counsel," she said.

"Legal counsel?" I said, popping a donut in my mouth. "For what?"

Even with trouble lurking, I can still find time for a donut.

"Because the lease has fallen into your hands, you are obligated to represent your species at the Halls of Universal Justice."

"Uh-oh." It was probably supposed to fall into the hands of a grown-up. Or maybe Bobby was supposed to find it. After all, he was far more qualified than I was to represent our species.

Even if it was a cosmic blunder, I wasn't about to say anything.

What I did say was, "Tula, I have a hard time believing an entire species can get evicted."

Tula picked up her leather briefcase. She pressed a black button right below the handle. We vanished.

We reappeared one second later in a hideous place that didn't contain a single color except drab gray. No yellows or blues or burgundies or lavenders. No sign of life: no trees, no birds, no fish or flowers, no streams or ponds or gardens or fields or forests, no grass, no soil. Nothing except cement. Every square inch of the planet was made out of cement. Even the most desolate desert on Earth was nothing compared to the nothingness of this dump.

It chilled me to the bone. "What happened?" I said. "Where are we?"

"This is Desoleen. This is where you and the rest of the humans will be sent if the eviction process is allowed to proceed," Tula said.

"Are you sure you don't want my brother?" I said. "He's a lot smarter than me. I think he's the one who should be here. There's a donut in my bedroom going stale right now 'cuz I'm not eating it. Do you really think that's fair to the donut?

"Sorry, Giles. The lease fell into your hands."

"But it was a mistake."

"It doesn't matter. It can't be reversed."

"We're about to get eaten by monsters," I screamed. "Can that be reversed?"

They were in a pack, flying right at us.

"They aren't monsters, Giles. They're Kundabons."

"What's a Kundabon?" I said.

"They are the guardians of Desoleen. They're like prison guards on Earth."

Each one was ten feet tall and albino. Their red eyes were triangle shaped, with black slits for pupils. Their dirty white wings were featherless, colorless, leathery and bat-like. Their thick rodent tails were longer than their towering bodies. Each tail had a giant knot at the end, turning it into a deadly ball and chain.

"Those aren't prison guards," I assured her. "Those are monsters. I know the difference between a guard and a monster. We Earth kids are really good at identifying monsters. It's our specialty. We can't fly. We can't shoot fire out of our fingertips. But we know a monster when we see one."

One of the Kundabons broke off from the pack. He smacked his tail on the ground and the knot at the end of the tail turned into a cage!

It dived right at me. I ducked, screaming.

"I dare you to try to escape," howled the monster, dangling his ghostly white cage over my head.

My lawyer met the monster's grim gaze fearlessly. "My client can leave whenever he wants," she said. "His species has not been evicted."

"No, but they will be." The Kundabon leered at me. "And when they do, I'll be waiting for you. I'll be waiting for the day when you try to escape from Desoleen. Do you hear me? I will follow you into black holes, through parallel universes. I don't care if it takes me one thousand years, I will hunt you down."

It flew back over by the other monsters.

"Oh, great," I said. "Not only is he ferocious and creepy, he's dedicated. This monster is committed to his job."

Another Kundabon came zooming down and swung its cage over my head. But it didn't try to stuff me inside it.

"Hey, Tula, you're sure they can't touch me?" I asked.

"I'm positive," Tula said.

"Hey, Kundabon," I yelled, "I'm not going in your smelly cage. 'Cuz we're not getting evicted."

"That's it, Giles," Tula said. "Don't give in to fear."

The Kundabons all turned their tails into cages. They rose high into the air, howling, banging their cages together, creating a ghoulish racket.

"You Kundabons are such losers," I screamed. "I'd rather be a cockroach than a Kundabon."

I was insulting a monster. Dude, I was insulting a monster.

Each cage had white bristly hairs on it. "Tula, is the cage part of a Kundabon's body?"

"Yes, Giles. The bars are made out of bone."

Bone? That freaked me out. I did not need to hear that. Whoever heard of a cage made out of bone? How can a cage be part of your body? How can you grow a cage just like you'd grow an arm or a leg?

I fixed my eyes on the closest Kundabon. One of the bars on his cage had a big hairy wart on it.

That did it. When you see a big hairy wart on a prison bar it kind of ruins your day. I didn't feel like teasing them anymore. In fact, what I really wanted to do was throw up.

"Tula," I begged, "get me out of here."

She pressed the black button on her briefcase and we returned to my bedroom in Manhattan.

I grabbed my lawyer's hand in a spasm of fear. "Will you help us, Tula?"

"I'll do everything I can," she said. "May I see the lease please?"

I handed it to her.

She unrolled the long parchment and examined it carefully. "Just as I thought. There's a clause here that may be helpful."

Well, at least she could read it. But did she have the power to get me out of this mess?

"Aren't you kind of young to be a lawyer?" I said.

"Kind of young?" she said. "What do you mean?"

"I mean you're just a girl."

"So?" She chuckled. "The next thing you'll be telling me is that I'm too blue." She gave me a suspicious glance. "You don't have anything against blue people, do you?"

"No," I said, "I think blue people are amazing. All I'm saying is that I want a real lawyer."

"If you don't want me, you can request another lawyer," she said glumly.

I thought she was cute, in an iridescent sort of way, but I certainly didn't want her knowing that, so I said, "I guess I'll take you. But don't screw up."

She rolled her eyes and grabbed her briefcase. "Are you ready?"

"Wait. Hold on a second. How long are we going to be gone? I don't want to freak Grandma out."

"Don't worry. I'll plant a hologram of you fast asleep in

bed. If she pops her head in the room, everything will seem perfectly normal."

The Giles hologram was quite convincing. A pillow was squashed between my legs, Giles style.

Tula pressed the black button on her briefcase. A second later, we were standing outside the Halls of Universal Justice.

CHAPTER **SIX**

THE BUILDING was a platinum castle supported by pillars of mist. When I tapped on one of the pillars, my hand went right through it. "Tula, how can a pillar be made out of mist?"

"Giles, the things you can't grab hold of are stronger than the things you can."

Outside the entrance, a reporter with bubble-gum lipstick and a mushroom-shaped head was clutching a microphone. She spotted us and nudged her robot cameraman. "Look. The defendant has arrived." She stuck her microphone in my face. "Do you honestly feel that your species deserves to live on Earth after all the destruction you've caused?"

"Don't answer that," Tula said.

"No comment," I mumbled into the microphone.

Smiling nervously into the camera, I followed my lawyer up the steps, between the misty pillars into the Halls of Universal Justice.

A hush fell over the crowded courtroom when I walked down the aisle. The aliens watched me with a mixture of fear and fascination.

Tula and I sat down at a table up front.

You know how some buildings have ivy racing up the side to the roof? Well, this courthouse had ivy growing on the inside. It ran along all four walls. Bizarre birds nested inside it, phosphorescent toucans, bright orange pigeons.

The judge's desk, now unoccupied, was separated from the rest of the courtroom by a bubbling brook that gushed out of one wall and vanished into another. A quaint little steel bridge arched over the brook.

I wished all the cute girls in New York could've seen me, a hero striding through a courthouse-greenhouse. It was the most organic place I've ever been. It had the heartbeat of a thousand jungles.

Was this a glimpse of what Earth could've been or might yet be?

Shafts of golden light came slanting down through the glass ceiling. Each column of light swarmed with dust particles that made a weird whispering sound, like voices murmuring.

"Tula, who's making all that racket?" I asked.

She pulled a magnifying glass from her briefcase and handed it to me. I held it up to a shaft of light. The dust particles were in fact microscopic creatures, thousands of them. Their antennae were twice as long as their bodies. They dived and tumbled through the air, doing perfectly executed back flips and swan dives, waving to me.

"Who are they, Tula?"

"Pollendoozees."

"Are they our friendzees?"

"Absolutezees," she said, laughing.

I shifted my attention over to the steel bridge. It's not every day you see a steel bridge in the middle of a courtroom.

It looked just like the Brooklyn Bridge, actually. Weird.

"Hey, Tula," I said. "The bridge was over there a second ago. What's it doing over by the wall?"

"It moved."

"What do you mean it moved? Bridges can't move."

"This one can."

Like most steel bridges, this thing was covered with rivets. All of a sudden, one of the rivets turned into an eyeball. It stared right at me. Luckily I didn't scream. You're not supposed to scream in a courtroom. But bridges aren't supposed to have eyes either.

One by one, the bridge opened its hundred eyes.

"It's a Bridgeling, Giles," Tula whispered. "It sees everything."

A little Bridgeling crawled out from underneath the other bridge, which appeared to be its mother. The baby Bridgeling couldn't reach the other side of the brook yet. Every time it tried to arch over the water, it fell in. It climbed dripping wet onto its mother's back.

Just in case you were wondering, Bridgelings move by arching their backs like worms.

"Bridgelings can be used to cross rivers and streams," Tula said. "They also come in handy if you're trying to move between galaxies or travel through parallel universes. They're invaluable if you have to cross a black hole or if you're in a big rush to get from the world of logic to the world of magic."

My mouth didn't just hit the floor. It almost hit a neighboring star system.

"They're almost extinct," Tula said with deep sadness. "They were wiped out by evil things because Bridgelings serve only kindness. These are the last two Bridgelings in the entire universe. This courtroom is their sanctuary."

I felt like walking over to the Bridgelings and saying, "Don't worry, dudes. I'll protect you."

Suddenly there was commotion. A loud buzz of aliens gossiping erupted in the courtroom as Queen Mooby and King Zoodle shuffled down the aisle. A purple girl paraded in between them. She must've been their daughter because her nose was raised high in the air in an unmistakable display of imperial snootiness. She had mint-colored hair with slinky-sized curls. She wore a pink halter top and matching go-go boots. Her jeans, glittering with scales, looked as if they were made from the skin of a dragon.

I had a feeling that's who everyone was gossiping about.

"Mom," said the purple girl, "when can we move to Earth?"

"As soon as the humans get evicted, dear," replied the queen.

The girl breathed a sigh of relief. "Good. Our planet is such a dump. I'm embarrassed to show my friends where I live."

"Isn't Earth a dump?" asked a cyborg hanging out in the back of the courtroom.

"Not compared to our planet," said the purple girl.

The reporter with the mushroom-shaped head aimed her microphone at King Zoodle. "Your Excellency," she said, "you've taken most of the blame for the environmental degradation on your planet. Rebel forces are growing. Your popularity is at an all time low. Do you have any comment?"

The king gave a tense smile. "My popularity will sky-rocket when millions of my loyal subjects move to Earth. The rebels can stay where they are and rot, as far as I'm concerned."

The reporter turned her attention to the purple girl. "Princess Petulance, you're not in handcuffs. I almost didn't recognize you."

The princess chuckled. She knew how to handle the media.

"How does it feel to be the biggest juvenile delinquent in the entire universe?" asked the reporter.

"It feels really cool," said the princess.

Queen Mooby put her hand over the microphone and hissed at her daughter, "That's not what you're supposed to say. You're supposed to say 'I've changed my ways. I've grown up. I've finally matured.'"

"Jeez, Mom. Do you want me to lie? I thought honesty was a big deal in this family."

Princess Petulance sat down alongside her parents five rows behind us. I couldn't take my eyes off her. She had a pirate tattooed on her right arm. He slept on a hammock slung between two tattoo palm trees. His green belly rose up and down while he dozed off.

He was snoring. The tattoo was snoring!

"Hey, Tula," I whispered, "her tattoo is alive."

"So?" Tula said.

The pirate snored so loudly everyone in the courtroom could hear.

An ogre-size bailiff came over and nervously tapped the princess on the shoulder. Although he towered over her, his voice cracked with fear. "Miss, if you don't tell your tattoo to be quiet, I'll have to ask you to leave."

The princess gave him a nasty look. The ogre hurried away. The purple girl told her pirate to shut up. The tattoo pirate lifted his head up groggily from the hammock, grabbed a tattoo jug of rum and took a big swig.

Tula saw me gawking at the princess. "You don't think she's cute, do you?"

I didn't answer.

"Do you?" Tula said, elbowing me in the ribs.

"No," I said.

Tula breathed a sigh of relief. Was she jealous? I think she was. I never made a girl jealous before. It was so cool!

"So tell me, Princess," said the reporter, "what changes will you make to Earth when you move there?"

"I'm turning Central Park into a mall," she said proudly. "I'm filling the Long Island Sound with bubble bath."

"Won't it poison the marine life?" asked the reporter.

The princess shrugged. "More room for my rubber ducky."

"What else will you do?" asked the reporter.

"I'm building a mile-high sand castle in the Sahara Desert," said the princess.

"What if it collapses in a wind storm?"

"That's precisely the point. All the prisoners tied up inside it will be crushed to death. All those who tried to dethrone my father. All those who said I don't look good in jeans. Death by sand castle. That's much more original than death by firing squad, don't you think?"

Jerry pranced into the courtroom. He murmured something to Princess Petulance, who nodded in agreement and glared at Tula with murderous hatred.

Tula leaned over and whispered in my ear, "She'll stop at nothing to get Earth, Giles. Absolutely nothing."

"Hey, Giles," Jerry said, "isn't Desoleen beautiful?"

I tried to ignore him.

"And those Kundabons," he said. "They're so charming."

Both Bridgelings stared at Jerry. Even the baby thought he was a loser.

"All rise," proclaimed the bailiff.

Everyone in the room flew up to the ceiling, except Tula and me.

"Take hold of my briefcase," Tula said.

I grabbed the handle and rose up in the air alongside her. When your lawyer can help you levitate you know you've got good representation.

Down below, a door opened. The judge emerged. It looked as if he was made out of pure crystal. He walked across Mama Bridgeling to get to his desk, careful not to step on Junior along the way. He made a melodious tinkling sound like wind chimes as he moved. He was a crystal being, transparent but not invisible. I mean, there he was. Stuff flickered inside him, gold and silver lights that were the suggestion of eyes and a mouth. He was an awesome shimmering presence who commanded the entire room without saying a word. When he finally spoke, his voice was kind yet mighty. "Should the humans be allowed to continue their stewardship of Earth? This is the question we must now ponder."

Stewardship? What the heck was that?

Tula and I sank slowly back to our seats, along with everyone else.

The judge signaled the alien prosecutor to deliver his opening statement.

The prosecutor stood up and cleared his throat. "Your Honor, we, the citizens of the universe, demand that the humans be evicted from planet Earth."

The crowd exploded. Jerry cheered the loudest.

"Order in the court," the judge demanded.

"Your Honor," continued the prosecutor, "they have violated one thousand, two hundred, seventy-three clauses in the lease."

"That's alotta clauses," I whispered nervously to Tula.

"Look what they have done to that beautiful planet," boomed the prosecutor. "Millions of gallons of oil spilled into the Gulf of Mexico. We can't even begin to measure the damage done to the fish who inhabit those waters. And that's just the beginning. There isn't one body of water or one piece of land on Earth that isn't contaminated. Thanks to human-kind, it's one of the dirtiest planets in the galaxy."

The prosecutor glared at me, as if it was all my fault.

Jerry jumped out of his seat and yelled, "Get rid of the bums."

"Order in the court," repeated the judge.

The many of eyes of mother Bridgeling and her baby were all bearing down on me.

The prosecutor sat down, twirling his antennae, proud of himself.

Tula rose calmly out of her seat and approached the bench. "Your Honor, I wish I could say that the disastrous oil spill was the only mistake the humans have made. But it isn't. They have committed other blunders. In doing so, they have violated more than one thousand different clauses in the lease. However, I would like to direct your attention to one clause in particular, number fifty-one." Tula pulled out the ancient scroll. "It reads like this: 'Before they can be evicted, the ten-ants will be allowed to undergo one final test to prove that they're capable of changing their ways.'"

"That clause sucks," Jerry shouted.

The judge signaled to the ogre bailiff, who grabbed Jerry by his upside-down dreadlocks and hauled him out of the courtroom.

"Get your hands off me," Jerry insisted.

Tula's eyes remained fixed on the judge. "Your Honor,

the Elders were the ones who drew up this lease. It was they who inserted this clause. We can't dispute the wisdom of the Elders. They understood something about human evolution that we can't grasp. Once they lived in caves."

Jerry came barging back into the courtroom and yelled, "Now they live in Detroit. You call that progress?"

The judge ignored the commotion and gazed at me with his shimmering eyes. "As much as I may be appalled by the behavior of your species I cannot go against the wisdom of the Elders. You will be allowed to undergo one final test to see if you're capable of improving."

"They don't deserve it," bellowed King Zoodle.

"This is an outrage," insisted Jerry.

Princess Petulance stood up and screamed, "You can't do this. It is my destiny to rule that planet. And besides, I already picked out wallpaper for the Central Park Mall."

The judge didn't hear any of it. He focused only on me, Giles. "As I was saying, young man, you and your species will be allowed to undergo one final test."

A rhyme popped into my head, right there in the Halls of Universal Justice.

> *My quest*
> *is a test.*
> *The test*
> *is my quest.*

That's how it is with poetry. It just pops into your head.

The judge continued. "Your test shall be . . ."

We all waited breathlessly.

"You must clean up an island," said the judge.

An island, I thought to myself. Cool. I get to hang out on

a tropical island for a couple of weeks. Cleaning it will be no problem. Islands aren't that big. What's there to do except pick up a few coconuts? I can surf all day, munch on mangoes and papaya. Maybe I'll even get a pet monkey or a parrot to keep me company. Sounds good to me.

"You Honor," Tula said, "does the island have a name?"

"Yes," said the judge. "Manhattan."

I almost fell out of my chair. "Manhattan? Did you say Manhattan? You want me to clean Manhattan?"

CHAPTER SEVEN

"**THAT IS CORRECT,**" said the judge.

"How can I clean Manhattan? I can't even clean my room."

"Your Honor," Tula said, "I understand that you want to give the humans a real challenge. But don't you think this is going overboard?"

"Not at all," replied the judge.

Tula took a deep breath. She placed her hand reassuringly on my arm and looked up at the crystal being. "Your Honor, how much time will my client be given to accomplish this task?"

"Twenty-four hours."

This time I did fall out of my chair. "Twenty-four hours? You want me to clean Manhattan in twenty-four hours?"

"The test will begin on Saturday night at the stroke of midnight," explained the judge. "It will end on the stroke of midnight on Sunday. It is currently Tuesday evening on Earth. That gives you four days to prepare for the challenge."

"It'll take a miracle to clean Manhattan in one day," I said.

The judge smiled. "Giles, you're a human child who hates going to the mall. That's a miracle itself."

"What about the other boroughs, Your Honor?" asked Tula. "Brooklyn? The Bronx?"

"Just the island of Manhattan," he explained. "That will be sufficient."

"The Hudson River?" asked Tula.

"No. That couldn't possibly be done in twenty-four hours. But hopefully the momentum of this challenge will inspire New Yorkers to decontaminate the surrounding waters."

"Your Honor, can you please give us a more precise definition of cleaning up Manhattan?" asked Tula.

If you wanted a precise definition of going insane, all you had to do was take one look at me.

"The streets must be made immaculate," said the judge. "Eliminate all graffiti from the buildings and subways. Dramatically improve the air quality. Restore the island to its original splendor, the way it looked when the native Americans inhabited it."

"You mean get rid of all the skyscrapers?" I asked.

"No. But make it a place where all life-forms can thrive. Prove, beyond the shadow of a doubt, that your species is capable of healing the planet." Something of a sly smile passed across his crystal face. "And along the way, add five million more leaves."

"In one day?" I yelled.

The judge nodded.

I rolled my eyes. "Are you kidding me?"

"Not at all," said the judge.

"Your Honor, if I planted fifty thousand trees they wouldn't sprout leaves overnight. It'll take years."

"You have a clever lawyer," he said. "You'll figure something out."

Luckily I had a great idea. I leaned over and whispered to Tula, "We can steal all the trees from New Jersey."

"Nobody's stealing anything, Giles," she said.

"It's hopeless, kiddo," Jerry cackled, getting chased around the courtroom by the ogre bailiff. "Start packing for Desoleen."

"Your Honor," Tula said, casting a suspicious glance at Jerry and the princess, "there are many beings throughout the galaxy who would love to see the humans fail. What's to stop them from dumping trash in Manhattan after my client has cleaned it all up?"

"Good question," replied the judge. "I have a placed a force field over the island that will make interplanetary littering impossible. You only need to worry about the bottles and cans and newspapers the humans have tossed onto the streets."

My mom and dad would figure something out. They were brilliant. And rich. "Hey, Judge," I said, "can I get my parents to help me?"

"No," said the judge. "If you tell your mother or father or any other adult, your species will immediately be evicted. The adults had their chance to save the planet and they failed. The fate of your species rests on your young shoulders."

"Can my client tell other children, Your Honor?" Tula inquired.

"He must do it on his own."

Tula threw her blue hands in the air. "Your Honor, this is extremely unfair."

I think the judge got mad because he turned dark red, like a ruby.

"I ask you to please have mercy," Tula said softly.

The judge returned to his normal clear color. "All right. All right. He can tell three other children."

"What happens if I tell more than three?" I asked.

"Then you automatically fail the test." Light danced inside him. "When the twenty-four hours has elapsed, I will personally walk the streets of Manhattan to determine if you have passed the test."

I remembered something extremely important. I was too embarrassed to say it in front of everyone, so I got up and headed toward the judge. Mama Bridgeling was feeding something to the baby. I didn't want to bother them, so I leaped over the stream. Luckily, I didn't fall in. I whispered in the judge's ear. "Your Honor, I've got a big problem. I'm supposed to be taking care of my grandmother. I gave Grandpa my word of honor."

"I am aware of that responsibility, Giles," the judge whispered back.

"You are?"

The judge nodded.

When Grandpa was sick we took him to the Grandpa Repair Store. That's what we called the hospital. Nikki came up with that word. They specialize in fixing grandpas. She'd tell the limo driver, "Take us to the Grandpa Repair Store please."

The Grandpa Repair Store kept Grandpa alive for three months. Then he got real bad. One day I was alone with him in his hospital room. He was hooked up to half a dozen machines.

"Giles," he said, "I want you to promise me something."

"Sure, Grandpa," I said.

"I want you to promise me you'll take care of Grandma when I'm gone. I'm very concerned about her. I don't think she's going to handle this very well. You need to take care of her while she's taking care of you. Will you do that for me, Giles?"

"Yes, Grandpa."

I didn't feel like bawling my head off in the middle of the Halls of Universal Justice but I was pretty darn close. I bit my upper lip and stared at the judge. "Your Honor, I don't see how I can take care of Grandma and clean Manhattan at the same time."

"Giles," whispered the judge, "think of the Earth as your other grandmother. She's sick. She's very ill. She needs to be healed."

I leaped back over the stream, went to my seat, and sat down.

"Court is adjourned," declared the judge.

"All rise," roared the bailiff.

We all rose to the ceiling. The crystal being walked across the Bridgeling and left the room.

As soon as Tula lowered us back down, Princess Petulance came prancing in our direction. "Good luck, Giles."

Tula rolled her eyes. "Like you really mean it."

"How do you two know each other?" I asked.

"Tula and I went to boarding school together," said the princess.

"Until you got kicked out for trying to chop off the math teacher's head," Tula said.

"I don't know what went wrong," said the princess. "I'll tell you. They don't make guillotines like they used to." She ran her fingers through her hair. "Don't freak out, Giles. I was just trying to scare him so he'd give me an A in trigonometry."

"What about the time you bit off that waiter's nose at the diner?" Tula said.

"He served me cold chili fries."

"So you bit off his nose?" I said.

"I hate cold chili fries." She giggled. "What's the big deal? He was a Martian elf. Their noses grow back in a couple of days. I never would've done it otherwise."

"Sure you wouldn't have," Tula said. My lawyer burst out laughing. "Hey, Princess, tell Giles about the time you tried to walk across a Bridgeling."

"What happened, Princess?" I asked.

A horrified look crept onto her royal face.

"She got turned into a dung beetle," Tula said. "She spent an entire semester crawling around inside her locker."

The princess was seething. Her pirate whipped out a miniature cannon, aimed it at Tula and was about to light the fuse.

"I wouldn't do that if I were you," Tula calmly told the tattoo, gripping the handle on her briefcase.

The pirate put out the match and wheeled his cannon dejectedly up the collarbone of Princess Petulance.

"It's so unfortunate what happened to the Bridgelings," the princess said with the fakest sympathy you ever heard. "There used to be thousands of them."

The two girls stood toe to toe like gorgeous gladiators.

Tula turned around, and strode through the door into the judge's office, waving to the baby Bridgeling.

The princess glared at her. "She's such a goodie-goodie. Just like Bobby."

How did she know Bobby?

"I hate goodie-goodies. Don't you, Giles? They think they're better than everyone. They're always rubbing it in your face." She smiled at me. "You're not a goodie-goodie. Are you, Giles?"

Her pirate tattoo stood up on her shoulder and saluted me.

"What's he saluting me for?" I asked. "I'm not on your team."

"Not yet you aren't," she said, sauntering away.

CHAPTER **EIGHT**

I WAS ALLOWED to tell three kids about the quest. The first one to get the big news was Nikki. I told her as soon as my lawyer got me back to New York City.

I poked my head out of my bedroom, made sure Grandma wasn't around, and led Tula down the hallway into my sister's room.

"Hey, Nikki," I said, "check out the blue girl."

Nikki took one look at Tula and dropped her violin. Tula caught it deftly before it hit the floor. She handed it back to Nikki. My little sister's hands trembled so badly she couldn't hold it, so Tula laid it gently in its case and smiled at the petrified six-year-old. "Aren't you the famous violinist?"

"I'm not famous," Nikki mumbled.

"She's an author too," I added. "She's writing a book called *How to Eat a Meatball*."

"I've always wanted to know how to eat a meatball," Tula said. "We don't have pasta on my planet."

"It's about ice cream," Nikki said.

"A book about ice cream called *How to Eat a Meatball*," Tula said. "It sounds splendid."

Nikki turned to me. "Giles, there's a blue girl in my room, talking about *How to Eat a Meatball*."

"I know, Nikki. Her name is Tula. She's our lawyer. She's here to help us."

"Help us do what?"

I told Nikki the whole story. Surprisingly it all made perfect sense to her, probably because she was so young. The younger you are the easier it is to understand the important things in life. The only thing Nikki couldn't believe was that I was keeping this a secret from Bobby.

"Giles, Bobby's the only kid I know who could figure out how to clean Manhattan in one day."

"Thanks, Nikki. It's nice to know you have faith in me."

"I'm sorry, Giles. It's just that . . ."

"I know. Bobby is smarter than me."

"He's smarter than me too, Giles. He's the smartest kid on the planet."

"Well, I've got other people I'd rather tell," I said. "Like Toshi and Navida."

Nikki threw herself into Tula's arms. "Tula, don't you think he should tell Bobby?"

"Absolutely," Tula said, stroking Nikki's hair, giving me a nasty look.

Snubbing my brother may not have been the most rational thing in the world. But would you be rational if you'd just hung out with Pollendoozees? I knew one thing for sure. If Bobby found out he'd try to take control. This was my quest. For once in my life I was going to be the star of this family.

We heard footsteps in the hallway. Tula popped open her briefcase and dived inside. She leaped into her briefcase! The briefcase slammed shut just as Bobby threw open Nikki's bedroom door.

I stepped in front of the briefcase, hiding it from Bobby's view.

He was carrying a fancy leather-bound notebook. He showed us the cover.

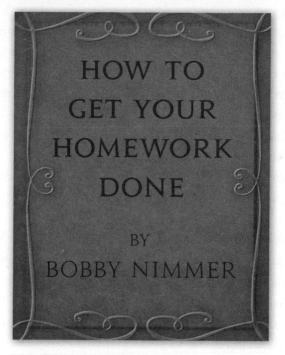

HOW TO
GET YOUR
HOMEWORK
DONE

BY

BOBBY NIMMER

He waved the notebook in my face, fanning me with a gust of wind that reeked of arrogance, the worst form of big brother pollution.

"I'm about to begin the final chapter of my literary masterpiece," he said. "This is like Dickens sitting down to write *A Tale of Two Cities*. Interrupt me and I'll kill you."

He slammed the door on his way out.

"Nikki, if Bobby is this cocky now just imagine what he'd be like if he saved the planet," I said.

Nikki pondered it for a moment. "Maybe we can pull this off without him."

"Of course we can. We've got the best lawyer ever. Did you see what she just did?"

The briefcase opened by itself. Our lawyer climbed out. Before we could ask her how she did it, Tula dived back into the briefcase. The bedroom door flew open. This time it was Grandma. I nudged the briefcase underneath the bed with my foot.

"Hi, Grandma," I said.

Grandma eyed us suspiciously. "What are you two up to?"

"Nothing, Grandma," Nikki said.

Grandma sniffed the air. "I smell mischief."

"What does mischief smell like, Grandma?" I asked.

"Like burnt pot roast."

"We weren't cooking any pot roast, Grandma," I assured her.

"I don't even like pot roast," Nikki said.

She kept sniffing. "I smell mischief. You two weren't planning on interrupting your brother in the middle of his writing, were you?"

"Yes, we were," I said. "You caught us, Grandma. We were just getting ready to go bother him."

My sister and I exchanged a sly glance.

"You leave your brother alone."

"We can't pull anything with you around, Grandma," I said.

"Don't forget it."

As soon as she was gone, I pulled out the briefcase and popped it open. "Tula?"

"Come on in," she said.

I stuck my head inside the briefcase. I felt as if I was peering into a magic cave. A cozy room revealed itself, roughly the size of my bedroom. It was Tula's office. If I had tried to jump down into it I would've broken my neck. The office walls were lined with bookshelves. A wooden ladder like the kind you see in libraries leaned against the far wall. It came swinging toward me. I climbed down it. Nikki followed.

"OK," Tula said. "If you're not going to tell Bobby then we need to move forward without him. Give me your cell phones."

We handed her our smart phones. She planted a microchip inside each of them.

"This will enable you to contact me up to five-hundred-million light years away. However, you won't be able to reach me when I'm in court. All electronic devices must be turned off inside the Halls of Universal Justice. Judge's orders."

"Why would you have to appear in court without me?" I asked.

"I have other cases."

"What do you mean you've got other cases? Don't you think this is important? Humankind is about to get evicted!"

"Giles, there are other species out there facing annihilation. I've got forty-four other cases."

"Forty-four?" Nikki said.

"Don't worry," our lawyer assured us. "I love a heavy workload."

"But will you have enough time for us?" Nikki asked.

"Of course I will. We just need to stay focused and take care of business."

That made me nervous. Being focused was not exactly one of my strengths.

"Nikki, you go practice your violin," Tula said. "Your brother and I have to go take care of something."

"How can we clean Manhattan with a violin?" I asked.

"Just trust me," Tula said.

Nikki scooted back up the ladder out of the briefcase into her bedroom.

Tula checked her watch. "Time to go, Giles. You and I have an appointment with Dr. Sprinkles."

"Who's that?"

Tula grinned. "You'll see."

I had to admit. My lawyer had a great smile.

She pressed a button on the side of her desk.

Suddenly we were standing on an asteroid. There was nothing on it except a glass slipper. I mean a really big glass slipper, longer than a football field, taller than a pine tree.

"Hey, Tula," I said, "the lady who owns that shoe must have really big feet. I wouldn't want to see one of her toenails."

"Giles, that shoe isn't for wearing."

"Then what's it for?"

"It's a building," Tula said.

She was right. It was a laboratory stuffed with machines, all pulsing and blinking inside the giant glass slipper. A golden flag billowed on top of the slipper-shaped lab. It read: THE ROYAL FEDERATION OF UNIVERSAL SCIENCE.

We walked up to the front door. Tula rang the bell.

A lady alien answered it. She was four feet tall. Her upper half was bloblike—not a giant blob, just a decent amount of gold jelly. Her round face, wedged in the middle of the jelly, had two big brown eyes like scoops of chocolate ice cream. She wore a blond wig and had pretty legs, which were obviously not real. I could see the bolts at the top. I don't know if she was trying to impersonate a human to make me feel at home or if she had watched too many Marilyn Monroe movies. I think it was the movies because she kind of sounded like Marilyn too.

"Tula, darling. How wonderful to see you." She gave me a pleasant blob smile. "You must be Giles."

"That's me."

"Please allow me to introduce myself. I am Dr. Melissa Sprinkles."

When she spoke, her ice cream eyes started melting. Was she crying? No, they weren't tears. Her eyes were sliding down her face! So were her nose and mouth. Her entire face slid from the top of her body down to the middle. She was a dainty blob with blond hair and a moveable face. Aliens are hard to describe but that pretty much sums her up.

"Tula told me about your quest so I could assist you on your noble cause." She led us inside. This blob wore black high heels that clattered on the marble floor.

I tripped over a shoebox.

"Watch your step, Giles," warned Dr. Sprinkles.

That wasn't easy. Shoeboxes were scattered all over the floor.

Dr. Sprinkles blushed. Her gold blobness turned flamingo colored. She straightened her wig. "As you can see, Giles, I have a thing for shoes. It's a weakness of mine. Well, not really a weakness. More like a strength. You see, I think up most of my inventions when I'm out scouring the universe for bargains. I came up with this idea when I was buying a pair of red pumps just the other day." She pressed a button on the wall. "Take a look, Giles."

A hologram of Manhattan appeared on top of her desk. In the hologram, paper was being sucked up off the streets and turned back into trees.

Dr. Sprinkles grinned with deep alien pride. "A machine that transforms paper and paper by-products back into trees. The logging industry in reverse."

"Whoa!" I got so excited I ran laps around her desk. "I can do it! I can do it! I can add five million leaves in one day!" I grabbed one of her stubby blob arms and shook it madly. It felt as if I was shaking hands with butterscotch pudding. "Dr. Sprinkles, the scientists on my planet are all pathetic compared to you."

Her face headed north. Occasionally the left eye would go in one direction while the right eye followed the mouth and nose in another, but most of the time they all stuck together. "Giles, this technology is not as sophisticated as you might think. Your government could've come up with it long ago if they didn't spend all their money building bombs."

"Do you really think so?" I asked.

"Absolutely. This is all basic stuff. Take Big Daddy for example."

"Who's Big Daddy?"

"He's your android."

"I've got an android?"

"His specialty is cleaning dirty planets." Dr. Sprinkles directed my attention back to the hologram. A street cleaner appeared, walking the streets of New York, wearing blue overalls, picking up bottles and cans. A perfect android disguise.

"Dr. Sprinkles," I said, "I'm sure that's one amazing android. But how can one droid clean the streets of Manhattan in twenty-four hours?"

"Good question, Giles. Your android is made out of recycled materials. He has the ability to reproduce."

"What do you mean?" I said.

"He will go around the city, picking up glass and plastic along with paper and paper by-products. The glass and plastic will be melted down and absorbed directly into the android. When he has reached full capacity, he will split in half and create another android."

In the hologram, Big Daddy went into a stall in the men's

room at Grand Central Station. A second later, two androids came out.

"That's the coolest thing I've ever seen," I said.

"Within two hours you'll have an army of one thousand androids cleaning the streets of Manhattan, sucking up paper, turning it back into trees." In the hologram, an android's chest opened up. The machine that turns paper back into trees flew into it. The android closed up, hiding its precious secret. "Half the androids will be male, half female," said Dr. Sprinkles.

"Will they all look the same?" I asked. "That might freak out some adults in New York City. They'll know something's up and we'll automatically fail the test."

"Don't worry. They will vary in appearance according to the kind of recyclables their parent picked up. For example, if a droid picked up a plastic six-pack ring, its child will have curly hair."

Her face spun figure eights around her body. You really had to stay focused when you were talking to her.

I gave her a high-five. "You know what, Doctor. If you can keep coming up with inventions like that, I say go buy some more shoes."

"There aren't any shoes left in this star system," Tula said, rolling her eyes. "She bought them all."

"Where did you get your shoes, Tula?" Dr. Sprinkles asked, eyeing my lawyer's gold high-top sneakers.

"I forgot," Tula said, trying to hide her feet.

"What size are they?" asked Dr. Sprinkles.

"They wouldn't fit you," Tula insisted.

"Let me try them on," said the doctor.

"No," Tula said with a small smile.

Dr. Sprinkles gave up and wrapped her stubby arms around Tula affectionately. Tula nuzzled her blue face up against the doctor's quivering consistency. You could tell they adored each other.

"Giles, your lawyer is an angel. She kept me from going to jail half a dozen times. You see, I have a tendency to be rather naughty."

"That's an understatement," said Tula.

"I've been to New York a couple of times to conduct experiments," said Dr. Sprinkles. "I was appalled by all the graffiti. If you want to pass the test then we'll have to get rid of it."

"How, Dr. Sprinkles?"

"With your flyplane."

"What's a flyplane?" I asked.

"It's a miniature spacecraft shaped like the housefly common to your planet."

In the hologram a housefly moving at supersonic speed, shooting a laserlike cleaning solution from its mouth, erased all the graffiti off an entire New York City building in thirty seconds.

"Dr. Sprinkles, I love it. But if it's the size of a normal housefly how am I going to fit in it?"

"With your S/U."

"What's an S/U?" I asked.

"A shrinker/unshrinker."

"You mean I'll be able to shrink myself down?" I said.

"Of course you will," she said.

I ran laps around the desk again. I gave Dr. Sprinkles another high-five.

"And, Giles, that's only the beginning. I've got more surprises in store for you."

Tula wasn't quite as excited as I was.

"This is all amazing," she said. But why are we only seeing holograms? Where's the real thing?"

The doctor quivered terribly. "I'm not finished yet."

"Dr. Sprinkles, you promised me they would be ready by tonight."

"Now, Tula, it's not my fault. I had a very busy day today."

Tula frowned. "I know what that means. There was a shoe sale."

"I do have one extraordinary contraption ready to go, Giles," Dr. Sprinkles said guiltily.

"What is it?"

"Hey, Stanley," Dr. Sprinkles hollered. "Get in here."

A parking meter came rolling into the room.

"A parking meter?" Tula said, frowning.

"What does it do?" I asked.

"Well, it can move around and it can talk," explained Dr. Sprinkles.

"What else does it do?" I said.

"Nothing really. It was an early invention of mine. But at least it's finished."

"That's the lamest gadget I've ever seen in my life," I muttered under my breath.

The parking meter spat a quarter at me and said, "Watch it, bozo."

"When will the rest of the technology be completed, Dr. Sprinkles?" Tula asked. "Giles has only four days to prepare."

"By tomorrow afternoon."

"Are you sure?"

"I'm positive." Dr. Sprinkles gave me a hug. "Giles, you'll have everything you need."

"I sure hope so," I said.

"Don't worry. You humans will be staying on Earth for another million years, I guarantee it. Now let's have some fun. All the nearest shoe stores are closed by now. How about a party?"

"Now you're talking," said the parking meter.

"We don't have time," Tula said.

The doctor began texting madly on her cell phone. "Too late. I've already invited the guests. You have to stay. Giles can mingle with other citizens of the universe. He's an ambassador for his planet."

An ambassador and a superhero. Doesn't having a fly-plane qualify you to be a superhero?

(Hey, reader, if you know what the superhero qualifications are post them on my Facebook wall right away!)

CHAPTER NINE

DR. SPRINKLES TRIED to put on some lipstick for the party but her face kept moving around. It had a will of its own.

"If you don't stop right now," warned the doctor, "I'll give up trying to put on makeup and you'll look positively hideous."

Her face stopped. It didn't want to look positively hideous.

After she had prettied herself, Dr. Sprinkles pressed a button on the wall. The laboratory vanished and was replaced by a dozen mouth-watering buffet tables.

"Have something to eat, Giles," she said.

"Thanks. I'm starving." I dashed over to the closest table. The table had feet and ran to the other side of the room.

"Giles, not that buffet table," said Dr. Sprinkles. "That's specifically designed for people who are on a diet."

All the pizza was on that table, so I wasn't about to give up. This time I snuck up on it. Just as I was about to grab a slice, it took off running. This time it yelled, "No pepperoni for you, fat boy."

"I can catch it, Giles," said the parking meter, rolling frantically across the room. "Do you want me to catch it for you?"

"No, Stanley," I said. "I don't need your help."

"OK," said the parking meter sadly, giving up the chase.

Tula led me over to another buffet table. "As your lawyer, I strongly recommend that you tell your brother about the quest."

"I'm not telling him anything. This is my secret."

"Giles, a secret is like a caged lion," Tula said. "Just because you've got it locked up inside your heart doesn't mean it can't reach it's big old paw between the iron bars and scratch your eyes out."

She walked away. I tried not to let it bum me out. She didn't understand. If I told Bobby that meant either Toshi or Navida would have to get bumped off the team. I wanted them both.

I didn't know what to do. With Nikki on board, I was allowed to tell only two other kids. I couldn't tell Bobby, right? I sure hoped I was right. Not only was it the biggest decision of my entire life, it was maybe the most important decision in the history of humankind.

"Hey, Giles." Stanley beckoned me over to a buffet table that contained a bowl of quarters. "Would you mind sprinkling some salt on them?" he asked ravenously.

I grabbed the salt shaker and sprinkled it on the quarters.

"The only thing that stinks about being a parking meter is that I don't have arms."

I could think of about five hundred other things that would stink about being a parking meter. But I didn't tell Stanley that.

I fed him ten quarters. He groaned happily. "I love the taste of pocket change."

The other bowl on the buffet table contained hundreds of tiny iridescent cars and trucks. I grabbed a little green truck and popped it in my mouth. It dissolved on my tongue

into a jelly that was the single most scrumptious thing ever.
"What is this stuff?" I asked.

"Traffic jam," said Dr. Sprinkles.

I leaned over to examine the bowl. All the little cars and
trucks were moving around, bumping into each other. I heard
voices, angry voices muttering, "Hey, don't cut in front of
me," and, "Who taught you how to drive?" and "Don't be a
backseat driver."

I ate ten handfuls of it. It almost got my mind off my dilemma. Who should I pick for my team?

Toshi was a lock. He was my best friend. Your best friend
is always part of your quest. It's the golden rule of all adven-
tures. OK, he did ballet. But so what? Toshi really wanted to
be a professional hip-hop dancer. His mom was making him
take ballet first.

Who knows? I thought to myself. His dance moves might
come in handy.

Navida had her own eco-blog and worked on it tirelessly.
At some critical point in the quest I might need someone to
do some blogging. Navida was passionately committed to pu-
rifying the planet. No one would get more excited about cleaning Manhattan than Navida. She'd been waiting her whole life
for a chance like this.

But then I pictured Bobby grabbing me by the neck on the
cement dump of Desoleen after we'd been evicted. "I can't
believe you didn't tell me about the test. If I had been in
charge we never would've failed it."

And my dad, who never yelled, was yelling at me now.
"You chose Navida over your own brother? Whatever happened to loyalty, Giles? You didn't just betray your own
family. You betrayed the entire human race."

Millions of people trapped on Desoleen were glaring at

me. A Kundabon circling overhead hissed at me, "Way to go, Giles. I knew I could count on you."

I didn't know what to do. I tried not to worry about it. Instead, I ate traffic jam.

Guests started showing up for the party. The first to arrive were half a dozen one-eyed thumb things. They looked exactly like giant thumbs with an eye in the middle. They were extremely polite. If anyone tells you one-eyed thumb things have bad manners, don't believe them.

Then came the Upside Downers. There were two of them, a married couple. Their heads were down on the ground. Dozens of tiny caterpillar feet were attached to their skulls. That's how they walked around. This seemed perfectly normal to them, as if I was the one who was wrong side up. Their faces lacked eyes and a mouth, so it was a waste of time to try and talk to them by staring at the floor. What you did, and it took some getting used to, was focus on their bare feet, which were sticking high in the air.

A bright green eye with long gold lashes peered out of each big toe. Their noses protruded from their ankles. They spoke out of a slit in their knees.

"Giles," said Mrs. Upside Downer, "on our planet, an Upside Down mother will tell her child, 'Your bedroom is too clean. Go mess it up.'"

"Sounds good to me," I said.

"If you're in perfect health, doctors will rush you to the emergency room," said her husband.

"So if you're ever on our planet and an ambulance comes by, act sick or they'll put you on a stretcher," she warned.

"Let me write that down," I said, searching for a pen.

"Here's the best thing of all, Giles," said Mr. Upside Downer. "At Upside Down Junior High, if the teachers talk during class, the students make them stay after school."

"That's the way it should be," I said.

Suddenly I had a wonderful thought. Now that I'm an ambassador, do I have to go to school anymore? The Upside-Downers caught a whiff of the traffic jam and made a beeline for it.

Dr. Sprinkles opened a bottle of wine for herself and the other adults, but instead of drinking it, she poured the entire bottle on a large potted planet in the corner.

"Dr. Sprinkles, what are you doing?" I asked.

"I'm watering the wino tree."

A wino tree. I should've guessed. Any place that had one-eyed thumb things and Upside Downers would naturally have a wino tree.

The wino tree belched. It was the most musical burp I ever heard. Too bad I couldn't download it on iTunes.

I glided through the crowd, introducing myself. If only my parents could see me now. They'd be so impressed. They'd stop talking about Bobby forever.

My mom would run around town saying, "My son was chosen to save the planet."

And my dad would never again say, "My son Bobby is number one in his class." Instead, he'd say, "My son Giles is an intergalactic hero."

The more I thought about it the more convinced I was that I should tell Navida.

Dr. Sprinkles tapped a spoon against her glass. "Attention, everyone." The room went quiet. "Now, for the moment you've all been waiting for. Giles will recite a poem."

"What?" I blurted. "No one told me I had to give a reading."

"Please, Giles," said Dr. Sprinkles, her face moving counterclockwise.

How could I say no? The lady was about to give me an army of droids and a flyplane. The least I could do was provide some entertainment. And besides, I kind of liked the idea of Tula watching me perform. She was the cutest blue girl I'd ever seen.

I winked at her as I made my way toward a microphone in the center of the room. "This poem is called 'Pigeons,'" I said. I took a deep breath and cleared my throat.

"I feed them bread
to keep them from
pooping on my head."

The entire crowd burst into applause.

"Bravo!" yelled the one-eyed thumb things.

"That was practically Shakespearean," shouted Mrs. Upside Downer.

We were having the greatest time when suddenly things turned nasty. Things usually turn nasty when a lady giant shows up. She came crashing up through the floor, overturning a buffet table. She was thirty feet tall and had baseball bat–size fangs and lots of tentacles.

She was decked out in a plaid dress, thick makeup and silver earrings bigger than garbage can lids. She grabbed Dr. Sprinkles with a tentacle. "You stole my shoes!"

"I have no idea what you're talking about," said Dr. Sprinkles, dangling in midair, quivering like a bowl of Jell-O.

"I was at the mall," growled the giantess. "There was a shoe sale."

"So?" said Dr. Sprinkles.

"You snatched a pair of black sandals off the rack. I saw them first."

She had tiny feet for a giant.

"Honey," said the doctor, "it's the law of the jungle at a shoe sale."

The giantess bared her fangs. "Honey, it's the law of the jungle right now too."

"How did you find me?" asked the doctor.

"A realtor gave me your address."

"Jerry!" I yelled.

"I think that was his name," said the giantess, tossing me a business card.

The card belonged to Jerry. It was a hologram. A miniature 3-D Jerry smiled up at me and said, "Hi, I'm Jerry. Selling real estate is in my blood. I closed my first deal before I was even born. I rented my mother's womb to my twin sister for two thousand gakmas a month. Hire me to sell your house or condo. Satisfaction guaranteed."

I flung the card down on the ground and stomped on it.

The giantess was about to gorge on Dr. Sprinkles. If she got eaten, my species was in big trouble. The Eco-droids and the flyplane weren't finished yet. Without her gadgets I could never clean Manhattan in one day.

The doctor was inches away from the monster's mouth.

"Wait, you can't eat me now," said Dr. Sprinkles. "There's a poetry recital going on."

"What does that have to do with it?" asked the giantess.

"It would be impolite to the author."

The giantess glanced down at me. "Sorry, kid. She stole my shoes."

"Now, hold on a second," Tula said. "Do you have a permit to eat scientists? Rule Three-zero-forty-two in the intergalactic predatory handbook clearly states that a scientist may not be eaten without a permit."

"As a matter of fact I do," said the giantess.

Tula marched right up to the monster. "Show it to me."

"Where did I put that permit?" said the giantess.

"It's right here, Mommy," hissed a baby giant, emerging from a pouch in the mother's belly.

"Thank you, pumpkin." She handed the permit to Tula.

Tula examined it.

The baby giant, who was roughly the size of an automobile, sniffed Dr. Sprinkles, drooling. "Mommy, can I have her eyeballs?"

"Of course you can, darling."

"They taste better than a hot fudge sundae," said the baby monster.

"Can't we come to some kind of agreement here?" asked Dr. Sprinkles.

"Yes, the agreement is I'm going to eat you," said the giantess.

"This permit seems to be in order," Tula said calmly.

The lady giant unhinged its jaws and was about to gobble Dr. Sprinkles. Tula tapped on one of her tentacles. "What do you plan to do with the brain?"

"What do you mean what do I plan to do with it?" asked the giantess. "I plan to eat it."

"You're not allowed to eat the brain of a scientist from the Royal Federation of Universal Science," explained Tula.

"I'm so glad I paid my membership dues," mumbled Dr. Sprinkles.

The giantess seemed totally perplexed. "If I can't eat the brain then what am I supposed to do with it?"

"It must be shipped back to federation headquarters, where it will be re-inserted back into Universal Brain, from which all intelligence emanates," Tula said.

"OK," said the giantess. "I'll send it back."

"How will you store the brain when you carry it across the galaxy?" asked Tula.

"I'll put it in my handbag."

"Wrong. You'll contaminate it. A brain belonging to a scientist from the Royal Federation of Universal Science must be transported in a . . ."

"I have a better idea," roared the giantess, getting rather frustrated. She dropped Dr. Sprinkles and pounced on Tula. "Why don't I eat you instead?"

I was about to become lawyerless. Now I was really in trouble. But the girl was fearless.

"Do you have a permit for eating lawyers?" Tula said.

"No, but I have a mouth for eating lawyers. I have razor-sharp teeth also."

"Then you'll be sent to prison and your child will be raised in an orphanage," Tula said.

"I DON'T WANT TO BE AN ORPHAN!" screamed the baby giant.

"My pumpkin, an orphan? Never!" The lady giant dropped Tula and disappeared through the hole in the floor.

Dr. Sprinkles climbed up off the floor while her face spun mad circles around her body. "That was a close one."

"Party's over," Tula said. "Giles has a quest to embark

on." She cast a stern eye at the doctor. "Dr. Sprinkles, I want your word of honor that the Eco-droid, the flyplane and everything else Giles needs for his quest will be finished by tomorrow afternoon."

The blob placed her hand over her heart. "You have my word of honor."

"Good," Tula said.

The parking meter came rolling toward me. "Giles, let me come with you to Earth."

The last thing I wanted was a stupid parking meter.

"No, Stanley," I said. "You stay here and keep an eye on Dr. Sprinkles. Don't let her go shoe shopping. If she tries to go to a mall, spit a quarter at her."

"Will do," Stanley said. "You can count on me."

"I know I can."

"I'm behind you one hundred percent, Giles."

"That's good to know."

When Stanley went for a bowl of quarters, I grabbed Tula by the arm. "Come on, Tula. Let's get out of here before that parking meter comes back."

She pressed the black button on her briefcase. Instead of returning to my bedroom in New York City, we ended up in a chicken coop, surrounded by hundreds of chickens. I had feathers all over me. So did Tula. It was so cramped I couldn't even stand. And guess what? The chickens weren't happy we dropped by to say hello. They were clucking like crazy. One landed in Tula's puffy blond hair.

"They don't have chicken coops in Manhattan. Where are we, Tula?"

I'd never seen Tula so embarrassed. She read some GPS coordinates on the side of her briefcase. "Door County, Wisconsin."

"What are we doing here?"

"I'm sorry, Giles. I made a mistake. Sometimes I don't focus like I should. My mind gets scattered. I have so many cases, so much going on."

I knew just what that felt like!

"So you do make mistakes just like me. You're actually capable of screwing up." I sat down in the hay. "I'm so happy to be in a chicken coop. You have no idea how happy I am to be surrounded by chickens."

"OK, Giles," she said, rather annoyed. "You don't need to keep rubbing it in." She removed the chicken from her head. "Let's get out of here."

Until now, she seemed too perfect to ever date a mere Earthling.

Back in my bedroom, I bolted the door to keep Grandma out. Tula cleaned us both off with a wave of her briefcase. I couldn't have smelled better if I had taken fifty showers.

We fell asleep on my couch. When we woke up it was Wednesday morning.

"I'll be back in an hour," she said. "Staff meeting at my law firm."

She disappeared.

It was time to tell Toshi everything I knew.

CHAPTER TEN

WHENEVER TOSHI ORDERED a slice of pizza he got it with quadruple extra cheese. I respected that. How can you not respect a kid who gets quadruple extra cheese?

He lived with his mom on the eighteenth floor of our building. A nanny took care of him when his mom was on tour. Toshi's mother was one of the greatest modern dancers in the world. Whenever she performed in her native Japan they practically had riots. She wanted Toshi to follow in her footsteps. Their apartment had a sprawling dance floor, with mirrored walls and a ballet bar.

Toshi's mom and dad were getting divorced. His dad, a music producer, had moved to Connecticut. Toshi was devastated by it. That was one of the reasons I decided to bring him in on the quest. Saving the planet seemed a good way to stop dwelling on the fact that your parents are splitting up.

I sent him a text message as soon as Tula went to her staff meeting. Toshi was off getting a haircut. I waited for him for in the lobby of our building.

I bumped into Grandma on her way out the front door.

"Where you going, Grandma?"

"To see the hypnotist."

Grandma has had trouble sleeping ever since Grandpa

died. She's tried sleeping pills, everything you could imagine. Nothing has cured her insomnia. She got so desperate a month ago she hired a hypnotist but it hasn't helped. I thought he was ripping her off. That made me really mad. You want to become an archenemy of mine? Go mess with my grandma.

She kissed me on the forehead. "Please stay out of trouble."

"You can count on me, Grandma."

Ten minutes later, Toshi showed up. I yanked him into the elevator before anyone else could get on. "Toshi, I need you to help me save the planet from an alien invasion."

He jabbed the button for the eighteenth floor. "I have to rehearse."

"Toshi, this is no time for ballet."

"Giles, you don't understand. My mom will kill me if I don't practice my pirouettes."

The elevator door opened on the third floor. Buck got on. He was our age but already the size of an NFL linebacker. His dad was the building superintendent.

He grunted. "Well, look who it is. The poet and the dancer boy. What are you sissies up to?"

We didn't say anything. Getting stuck in an elevator with a bully is worse than getting stuck in a tree house with a big black snake. I wondered if I could just get Buck sent to Desoleen. Maybe I could talk to the judge about it.

He elbowed Toshi in the ribs. "I asked you a question. What are you sissies up to?"

"Nothing, Buck," Toshi mumbled.

Toshi was half my size. If I'm a shrimp then he was a rock shrimp. He was even more pickonable than I was. Toshi was the most pickonablest kid you ever met.

Buck grabbed Toshi by the throat and lifted him up off the floor. "I don't get it. Your ancestors were ninja and samurai. What's your problem? Oh that's right. You don't do kung fu. You do ballet." Buck cackled and let Toshi go.

Toshi crumpled onto the floor.

Buck's cackle turned into a long cruel laugh. "You don't have a black belt. You have a tutu."

Toshi was about to cry. I sure hope he didn't start bawling. He'd never hear the end of it. I had to do something. Out of nowhere a poem popped into my head.

"Hey, Buck," I said, "I just came up with a new poem. Wanna hear it?"

Still crouched on the floor, Toshi looked up at me as if I was insane. Normally the last thing I'd do is tell Buck about my poetry. But when you've hung out with the Upside Downers everything inside you goes topsy-turvy.

"Sure, Nimmer," Buck said. "Let's hear your stupid poem."

I cleared my throat.

> *"I'm thinkin'*
> *of buyin' a lion.*
> *I'll feed him bullies and jerks.*
> *That's how it works.*
> *I'm thinkin'*
> *of buyin' a lion."*

Buck got right in my face. "Nimmer, did you just threaten to feed me to the lions?"

"I'd never do that, Buck."

"Got any money?" he asked.

"I'm broke," I said.

"Sure you are. Your mom and dad are millionaires." He punched me in the stomach. I couldn't breathe. "Give me all your money and maybe I won't kill you."

He nailed me again in the stomach. I didn't feel so brave anymore.

"OK, OK," I said, wheezing, digging into my pocket, pulling out three twenty-dollar bills. "Take it."

He got off on the eleventh floor.

Toshi and I kept going up.

I was trying to regain my breath and Toshi was rubbing the back of his head when Tula climbed down from the escape hatch in the top of the elevator.

"You mean you were up there the whole time?" I said in shock. "Why didn't you help me?"

Toshi whimpered. "Giles, that's . . . that's . . . an alien."

"I loved your lion poem, Giles," Tula said.

That was no consolation.

"You saw him kicking my butt and you didn't try to help me? Some lawyer you are."

"Giles," Toshi said, trying to hide behind me, "who . . . who . . . is this blue girl?"

"She's my lawyer. I thought she was on my side. Obviously she's not." I was so angry. "Why didn't you chop off his arms and legs? You've got superpowers. Why didn't you sic your briefcase on him?"

"I would've resorted to violence, Giles," Tula said.

"Hallelujah!" I shouted.

"I wouldn't have been able to control my rage."

"And what's wrong with that?" I asked.

"Giles, listen," Tula said. "I made a pledge to live a life of nonviolence. It's as important as the pledge I took to never tell a lie. If I ever broke either one of those pledges I'd get kicked out of my law firm."

"A law firm that believes in honesty and nonviolence?" I said. "You really are an alien, aren't you?"

She ran a blue finger along the gold letters engraved on the side of her briefcase: KINDNESS FIRST. ALWAYS AT ALL TIMES. ALWAYS. "This is the motto of my law firm."

"I get that with animals. They're defenseless. But Buck sure as heck isn't."

"It doesn't matter, Giles," she said. "You must treat him the same."

"You mean I have to be kind to my enemies?"

"Especially your enemies," Tula said.

"Fine," I said. "I don't need your help. I . . . I just don't like people spying on me."

"Will someone please tell me how an alien got in the elevator?" Toshi said. "Someone needs to explain that to me right now."

"Toshi, how rude of me. My name is Tula. I've been chosen to . . ."

"She's been chosen to make a fool out of me," I said.

"I've been chosen to represent you, Toshi," she said.

"Represent me for what?"

"We're getting kicked off the planet," I said.

If I had known she was up there I never would've handed over the money without a fight.

When a girl you've got a crush on sees you at your weakest moment, life can't get much worse. It was more embarrassing than if I'd forgotten to lock the bathroom door and she'd walked in and caught me popping a zit on my face.

She'd never go out with me after this. Who would ever kiss a coward? Lawyers probably weren't supposed to kiss their clients anyway. Not that it mattered now.

"Who's getting kicked off the planet?" Toshi said.

"Our entire species," I said.

"This is really starting to freak me out," Toshi said.

"Don't worry, Toshi," Tula said. "The eviction process can be halted."

"You know what can't be halted?" Toshi said. "Ballet. If I don't practice ballet my mother will kill me. That's where I'm going right now. To practice ballet. I don't want to hear anything else about the end of the world." He stuck his fingers in his ears. The elevator doors opened. Toshi marched down the hallway. "You're not even a real alien. You're just some kid in a cool costume."

He threw open the door to his apartment.

Half a dozen aliens in all shapes and sizes were doing ballet, pirouetting up the side of a wall, somersaulting across the ceiling.

An alien ballet teacher hovered in midair, bellowing, "That's it, ladies. One, two, three, four . . . one, two, three, four . . ."

Toshi's mouth hit the floor. "What in the name . . ."

Decked out in a tutu and ballet slippers, Princess Petulance did a perfectly executed arabesque, upside down, hanging from the chandelier.

Tula rushed over to the CD player floating above the couch and turned it off. "You are not allowed to dance on this planet. My clients have not been evicted yet."

Petulance leaped down to the ground and glowered. "Shut up, Miss Goodie-Goodie."

"I'll get a temporary restraining order," Tula warned.

"OK, OK. If Giles wants us to leave we'll leave." The princess sauntered up to me with a flirty grin on her face. "Come on, Giles. How is one little ballet class going to hurt?"

"OK," I said. "You can do one class. Then you have to leave."

Tula yanked me off into a corner. "Why are you giving in to her?"

"It's like you said, Tula. Kindness first."

"That doesn't apply to her."

"You said it applies to everyone. Especially your enemies."

I didn't do it out of kindness. I did to make Tula jealous, to get back at her for allowing Buck to pound on me. I had another motive too. I didn't trust Princess Petulance. I knew she was plotting something. But what? If I hung out with her I might be able to figure it out. I might discover her weaknesses.

I didn't tell Tula that. I wanted her to be angry and jealous.

"Fine," she said. "I'm due back in court. Go waste your time, Giles. You have nothing more important to do."

"The test doesn't start till Saturday. What's the big rush?" I asked. "I always study the night before."

"You haven't finished building your team. But is that a priority? No. You'd rather hang out and play games." Tula sadly shook her head. "Unbelievable." She pressed the button on her briefcase and disappeared.

She did have a point there. I had to select the final member of my team. Bobby or Navida? I was still leaning toward Navida.

She and I were sort of a team already. We called ourselves the UNLs, the Urban Nature Lovers. Navida got the idea from her mom, who was a famous environmental lawyer. Navida learned so much from her mother she was practically a lawyer herself. That could be invaluable. If Tula was busy on another case, maybe Navida could handle the legal aspects. Best of all, Navida didn't rub being smart in your face. Not like Bobby.

There it was. Navida was the one.

I called her. She didn't pick up. I left a message on her voice mail. "Hi, Navida. It's me, Giles. I've got some big news. I mean really big news. Call me immediately. No, call me way before immediately. Call me half an hour before immediately. That's how important this is."

The ballet teacher was a huge floating creature, part robot, part moose. She was a flying refrigerator with antlers. Judging from the vile look on her face, I bet she had an aunt or an uncle who was a dragon. She roared at one her students, "How many times have I told you, Nancy? Don't eat the ballet bar."

Nancy was a shy, termite-like girl. "I'm sorry, Teacher," she mumbled, her buck teeth covered with splinters.

Toshi stared in horror at the pile of sawdust on the floor. "My mom's going to kill me."

He forgot all about that when the princess batted her eyelashes at him. "Please take ballet with us, Toshi."

This concerned me. I didn't want Toshi getting chummy with the princess.

"Listen, dude," I murmured in his ear. "I know you don't believe everything I've told you. But that purple girl is not to be trusted. Do you understand?"

"Got it," he said.

The ballet teacher hovered grumpily over a pair of legs propped up against the wall. "Whose legs are these?"

One of the alien girls raised her hand. "Mine, Teacher."

"How can you do ballet without any legs?"

"I'll use my tentacles."

"You most certainly will not," insisted the teacher. "Tentacles are only allowed in aqua ballet."

The girl put her legs back on and joined the rest of the

dancers, who had gathered over on the right side of the room to go across the floor. Across the floor is an exercise in which everyone dances from one end of the room to the other. Don't get me wrong. I'm not some geeky ballet expert, but when your best friend does it all the time you pick up the terminology.

"Whomever does a pirouette incorrectly will be eaten," the teacher announced. "Toshi, you go first."

Toshi turned in terror to the termite girl. "You can go ahead of me if you want, Nancy."

"No way," Nancy replied.

Toshi couldn't stop shaking. "Teacher, I . . . I have to use the bathroom."

"Do your pirouette first."

Toshi did a pirouette.

"Well done, Toshi," said the teacher.

Toshi almost fainted with relief.

My cell phone rang. It was Navida. I popped into the kitchen to be alone.

"Hi, Navida."

"What's your big news, Giles?"

"Here's the scoop, Navida. We humans . . ." Once I told her I could never tell Bobby.

Standing by the toaster oven, the strangest thing happened. I suffered a bizarre case of amnesia. I forgot about all the annoying stuff my brother's ever done to me and only remembered the good things, like the time he rescued me in the elevator. We were down in Miami, on vacation with my parents.

I snuck down to the hotel lobby in the middle of the night to get a Snickers bar from the candy machine. The elevator got stuck on the way back. Elevators don't work down in Florida like they do in New York. You never hear of people getting trapped in elevators in New York. We know how to make elevators. Our elevators are as good as our pizza. But anyway, I got trapped. To make matters worse, the alarm button didn't work. I was stuck in there for six hours.

No one could figure out where I was. They thought I'd been kidnapped. None of the adults even noticed an out-of-order elevator because the hotel had, like, twenty elevators. But Bobby noticed. He had a hunch I was trapped inside it and called the fire department.

What if I got trapped in a dungeon on the moon in the middle of the quest? I might need my brother. He'd be so grateful I made him part of the team he'd never tease me again.

The sound of Navida's voice snapped me out of my daze. "Giles, what's your big news?"

"Navida, I have to call you back." I hung up, determined to make my brother a part of the team.

Five seconds later, something unfortunate happened. I got a text message from Bobby. It said:

Dear Moron, I saw your book title on the dining room table. *You Can't Have My Planet, But Take My Brother, Please.*

Oh no. I left it there by mistake.

Here's what the rest of Bobby's text message said:

It was just a title page because a pea brain like yours couldn't possibly write a book. But if by some miracle you ever did write one and insulted me on the cover, then I would have to exterminate you. After three or four months of torture. Yours truly, the Ultimate Genius.

My amnesia ended. I vowed never to tell that egomaniac about the quest. But I was way too embarrassed to call Navida back.

I trudged back out onto the dance floor.

Petulance was in the middle of a pirouette. She leaped so high she banged her head on the chandelier.

The teacher growled, "Young lady, come over here."

"Do I have to, Teacher?" asked the princess.

"You most certainly do."

"I hate getting eaten by the teacher," muttered the princess.

"You mean you've been eaten before?" asked Toshi.

"Dozens of times. She spits me out at the end of class. My tutu gets covered with gunk. How am I supposed to look good with gunk all over my tutu?"

Dragging her feet, she walked over and got gobbled up by the teacher.

"All right now, class," said the teacher. "Let's work on our leaps."

Toshi screwed up on a cabriole and got eaten. I had a feeling he did it on purpose. Right before getting swallowed, he winked at me and said, "Later, Dude."

"Toshi, no," I yelled. "It's a trap."

Too late. He was gone. Petulance lured him to his death.

CHAPTER **ELEVEN**

IF A KID GOT MUNCHED ON could I replace him with a new team member? Was I allowed to tell a fourth child about the quest? It didn't matter now. My best friend got gobbled like a candy bar because of me. I never should've let the aliens do ballet. I should've stayed focused on the quest but I got distracted. I was allergic to concentrating. Just ask my teachers.

A minute later I got a text message. It was Toshi. For a second I thought they had cell phones in heaven. But the message said:

Hey, Giles, guess what? I'm texting you from inside the teacher's belly.

That was probably the weirdest place I ever got a text message from.

We're playing video games, Giles. There's a room in here. With a couch.

I shot him a text back.

It must be like Tula's briefcase, Toshi. She has an office in there.

At the end of class the teacher spat them both out.

"That was the funnest dance class ever," Toshi told me. "Aliens are cool. I hope they take over Earth."

"You wouldn't say that if you saw the Kundabons, Toshi," I said.

"Dude," he said, "open your eyes. Aliens are hipper than half the humans I know."

"I don't care," I said. "Dance class is over."

I got the teacher, the termite girl and the other dancers to leave. Only Princess Petulance remained. She wouldn't stop flirting with Toshi, and Toshi wasn't used to having cute girls flirt with him. The tattoo pirate dived off her shoulder into the palm of his hand and clipped Toshi's fingernails with his dagger. Toshi was spellbound. It made me squirm inside, especially when she said she had a secret to share with him and pulled him into the kitchen to keep me from hearing. I tried to follow them, but two alien guys appeared out of nowhere, blocking the door. They called themselves the GPPs, the Groupies of Princess Petulance.

The first guy was covered with cartoons and horror movies. It looked as if someone had peeled off his skin and replaced it with a some futuristic TV screen, something far beyond human technology, a screen that could bend and stretch like normal skin. A TV you could wear! A pair of surfer shorts was all he had on besides the TV, and each part of his body was playing a different show. A cartoon about a pot-bellied robot played on his shaved head.

This guy's name was Cable.

"I had a crush on the princess," he told me, lingering in front of the kitchen door so I couldn't get through. "She wouldn't give me the time of day. She said TV was only her love. So I had cinematic plastic surgery."

"Did it make any difference?" I asked.

"No," he said, "but at least she made me a groupie."

I hoped I didn't have to have cartoons on my nose to get Tula to kiss me.

The other goon had a head and a tail but no body. His name was Heads-or-Tails. The head resembled a wild boar's, with long gnarly steel tusks connected to a curly pink pig's tail. He bounced on the tail like a pogo stick.

"What happened to your body?" I asked.

"I had a weight problem," he said. "So I decided to have it removed."

"Did it work?" I asked.

"Heck, yeah. I lost nine hundred pounds in five minutes."

Heads-or-Tails looked foolish but there was something cunning about him, as if the pogo stick was merely an act to get you to put your guard down. He reminded me of one of those court jesters from the days of Henry VIII, a court jester clutching a dagger behind his back.

Meanwhile, I was dying to know what was happening in the kitchen. Toshi was still in there with Petulance and I couldn't get past these gays.

Suddenly, the princess marched out of the kitchen with Toshi by her side. She scowled at her two groupies. "What are you idiots doing? You're supposed to be worshipping me."

They fell to their knees in front of her.

Toshi jerked me into the kitchen and shut the door. "Hey, Giles, check this out. The princess said you and I won't have to go to Desoleen with the rest of the humans."

"What do you mean?" I asked.

"We get to stay here."

"Tula never said anything about that."

"That's because your lawyer's an idiot," Toshi said. He

grinned. "We kids will run the planet. I get Asia. You get Australia."

"Dude, what are you talking about?"

"Princess Petulance is giving you Australia, Giles."

"Are you serious?" I said.

"I am totally serious. All we have to do is fail the test."

The princess joined us in the kitchen. "Giles, I'm making you Prince of the Land Down Under."

I was speechless.

Would Bobby ever be jealous.

Like the Halls of Universal Justice, my palace would be filled with birds, rainbow lorikeets and jabirus sailing past my throne. Kangaroos with razor-studded boxing gloves would guard the entrance to my royal chamber.

Petulance was giving me an entire continent. How can you possibly say, "No, that's OK. I don't need a continent. I'd rather clean up the trash. Give it to someone else."

(Hey, reader, would you turn down a continent? Sure you would. Like I really believe you. I'm serious. I totally believe you. You don't need a continent. You'll take a new smart phone but not a continent. That sounds perfectly rational to me. I'm glad I got your input on this matter. It was really helpful.)

"Hey, Princess," I said, "can my grandmother stay on Earth with me?"

She chuckled cruelly. "You're a prince now. Princes don't whine for their grandmothers. They chop off heads and plunder neighboring kingdoms."

"What about my mom and dad?" I asked.

"No adults," the princess proclaimed.

"Well, at least my little sister, Nikki. She can stay, can't she? She can play the violin."

"I detest the violin," said the princess.

What good was a kingdom without my family?

"You guys are right," I said. "Who needs them?"

I didn't want them knowing I wasn't on their side. Suddenly I knew it was all a lie. If Petulance did let us stay on Earth, Toshi and I would end up being her slaves.

"I'll be right back, you guys," I said. "I have a map of Australia in my bedroom. I need to go get it. I want to study my kingdom."

They fell for it and let me leave the apartment.

I took the stairs, since I didn't feel like bumping into Buck in the elevator again. Tula was waiting for me in between the twenty-first and twenty-second floors.

"Tula, we've got a big problem. The princess turned Toshi into a groupie."

"I warned you. But would you listen to me?"

Someone was coming up the stairs.

"Come on," I said. "Let's go to my apartment before someone sees you. Grandma's gone."

We raced up to the penthouse. When we were almost at the top floor I froze. I heard Buck grunting. I opened the stairway door a crack. He was changing a lightbulb in the hallway.

"Buck's out there," I whispered.

"If he tries to pull anything, whack him with my briefcase," Tula said. "But don't hit him in the head. Do you promise, Giles?"

"I promise."

She dived into the briefcase. I grabbed it by the handle, whistling cheerfully. This was going to be so much fun.

"Hi, Buck," I said.

He climbed down off the stepladder.

"Nice briefcase," he said.

Before I could nail him with it, he snatched it out of my hand.

"Give it back."

He knocked me down with the stepladder and disappeared into the elevator.

"Great," I said. "Not only is Toshi a groupie, now Buck's got Tula."

My team keeps getting smaller and smaller.

CHAPTER **TWELVE**

WITH NIKKI BY my side urging me on, I lingered outside Bobby's bedroom, fidgeting, getting ready to knock on the door. There was no way around it. I needed his help to get the briefcase back from Buck. Grandma was still seeing the hypnotist. And Tula was unusually powerless.

I sent her a text message a couple of minutes ago. Here's what I said:

Tula, maybe you should turn Buck into an insect so he won't tell anyone he saw an alien.

And she wrote back:

Giles, I'm the one who feels like a bug in a jar. I'm trapped inside this briefcase.

I texted right back:

How can you be trapped?

This was her depressing text:

The briefcase is a living organism, Giles. It feeds on positive energy like love and kindness. Buck has it in his possession. He is extremely

negative, full of bitterness and rage. Those dark forces have neutral-
ized its powers. Basically my briefcase has shut down.

Her cell phone must've shut down too because I couldn't
reach her anymore. I had no idea what to do. Bobby would
figure out something. I had to tell him everything. It was
time. I knocked on his door. There's a sack in your soul that's
made for storing secrets. My sack was fuller than a backpack
crammed with every book in your locker. I was tired of lugging it around.

I knocked on his bedroom door again.

"Come in," he said.

Nikki and I entered.

He was sitting at his desk, typing on his computer.

"Bobby, I've got a big problem," I said.

"So do I," he said without looking up. "You."

"Bobby, listen to him," Nikki pleaded.

"OK, OK." He put his laptop to sleep. "What's your
problem?"

"Buck stole my briefcase," I said.

"What briefcase?"

"The one my alien lawyer gave to me."

"Your alien lawyer?" Bobby said.

"Her name is Tula," Nikki said. "She looks like the sky,
but without helicopters."

"Remember what I told you, Bobby?" I said. "How we're
getting kicked off this planet. Well, it's the truth. And the only
way to stop it is if we clean Manhattan in twenty-four hours."

"If who cleans Manhattan?" asked Bobby.

"Me, you, Nikki and Toshi. Toshi's been brainwashed by
the enemy. We'll deal with him later. First we have to get the
briefcase."

"First we have to call the National Doofus Society and tell them you made the honor roll."

"Oh yeah?" I said. "Take a look at this." I showed him the lease.

He examined it, handed it back to me. "Adam and Eve. What a joke."

"It's not a joke, Bobby," insisted Nikki.

"Just help us get the briefcase, Bobby," I said.

"Tell your alien lawyer to help you," he said.

"I can't."

"Why not?"

"She's trapped inside it."

"Your alien lawyer is trapped inside the briefcase?" he said.

"Her office is in there," I explained.

"I hung out in it, Bobby," Nikki said. "The couch is so comfy."

He scowled at me. "Giles, I could care less if you lost your mind but I have a big problem with you brainwashing Nikki."

"Forget it, Nikki," I said. "I told you he was a waste of time. We don't want your help, Bobby."

"Giles, we can't do it without him," Nikki said.

She was right.

"Bobby," I said, "just help us get the briefcase. Buck's got it. You hate Buck as much as we do. Wouldn't you just love to nail him?"

"That does sound rather appealing," Bobby said.

"Then you'll help us get it back?" Nikki said.

Bobby hesitated.

"Bobby, if you help me get it back I'll do anything you ask," I said.

"Anything?" he said.

"Anything."

He whipped out a pen and a piece of paper and wrote out a contract. "I want this in writing. I get half your allowance for the next five years."

"All right. All right," I said.

"Even when I'm at Harvard you'll mail me half your allowance every week."

"OK, OK," I said. "Now let's go get the briefcase."

"Even after *How to Get Your Homework Done* is a number-one best-seller and I sell the movie rights to Disney, and I'm a multi, multi—add a few more multis to that—millionaire, you still send me half your piddly allowance. Is it a deal?"

"It's a deal," I said.

I signed the piece of paper.

"OK," Bobby said. "Let's go get the stupid briefcase."

We took the elevator down to the basement. Bobby knocked on the superintendent's door.

The super answered on the third knock. He was in his typical miserable mood. "Whadda you want?"

"Excuse me, sir," Bobby said. "Buck stole my brother's briefcase. I'm sure you didn't raise your son to be a thief."

"Buck, get over here," yelled the super.

Buck lumbered out of his bedroom.

"Did you take his briefcase?" asked the super.

"Here, take the stupid thing," Buck said. "I can't get it open. I tried a drill, a baseball bat and it still wouldn't open."

This was a lot easier than I thought it was going to be. Just as Buck was about to hand it to me, his sleazy father grabbed it. "Wait, hold on a second. This isn't a kid's brief-case."

"It's mine. Give it to me," I demanded.

"If it's yours then how do you open it?" asked the super slyly.

"Yeah, Nimmer," Buck snorted. "Let's see you open it."

This was a big problem.

"OK," I said. "I'll open it. No problem. Just give it to me." He handed it to me. I tried to open it. It was locked. I was about to take off running but Buck read my mind. He cut me off. I really did have to open it.

I remembered what Tula said, how the briefcase responded to positive energy. So I tried to think positively. I remembered back when Grandpa was still alive. He and I were taking a stroll through Central Park with Grandma. All three of us were holding hands. Grandpa knew the name of every tree and flower we walked past. He and Grandma had had a flower shop over on Amsterdam Avenue for twenty-six years. Grandma knew all the names of the trees and flowers too but she liked to let Grandpa show off. There we were, the three of us, moving through the golden light of late afternoon. Grandpa was complaining, like he always did, that there weren't enough trees in Central Park. It needed twice as many trees. Three times as many. Me and Grandma were laughing. He was alive, alive, he was still alive. He and Grandma were hugging and kissing, still in love after fifty years. Still in love.

The briefcase began to open.

I felt like I needed to say something to impress Buck, so I hollered, "Abracadabrawithpepperoniandextracheese."

The briefcase opened wide. I immediately shut it so they wouldn't see Tula's office.

"Abracadabrawithpepperoniandextracheese?" Buck said. "What kind of password is that?"

"The right password," Bobby said, smiling at me. Even he was impressed.

But I wasn't finished yet. I was on a roll. "Hey, Buck, I bet I can fit Nikki in my briefcase."

"I bet you can't," he said.

"Would you care to put a little money on it?" I asked.

"I'll bet you a hundred bucks," his dad said.

"OK," I said. "It's a bet."

The super rubbed his hands greedily. "I'm gonna steal this little rich kid's money."

I opened the briefcase, picked up Nikki and calmly dropped her inside it.

"Later, dudes," she said, vanishing from sight.

I slammed it shut. "OK. Where's my hundred bucks?"

They were all flabbergasted, especially Bobby.

I've seen the super ticked off before but never as mad as when he had to fork over the cash. He slapped Buck on the side of the head. "It's all your fault. This never woulda happened if you hadn't stolen it in the first place."

Buck ran into his bedroom, whimpering. That was more precious to me than the hundred bucks.

I brought the briefcase back up to the penthouse while Bobby scratched his head. "Giles, how did you do that trick with Nikki? And where is she?"

I opened the briefcase. "Go ahead. Look inside."

Bobby peered inside.

Nikki waved up at him. "What's up, dude?" she said, sprawled out on the couch. "Come on down."

Bobby backed away. "I'm not going in there."

"Come on," I said. "Don't be a chicken."

"I'm not going in there."

He meant it. So Nikki and Tula climbed out into our living room.

Eyes bulging with fear, Bobby gaped at Tula's blue face. "You're a . . . you're a . . ."

"That's right," I said. "She's a lawyer."

"Your brother's a real comedian," Tula told Bobby.

When Bobby realized that Nikki and I weren't scared of Tula, he calmed down a bit.

"Aren't you kind of young to be a lawyer?" he said.

"Not where I come from," Tula said.

"What did you get on your SATs?" my brother asked.

I rolled my eyes. "The end of the world is at hand and he's worried about his SATs."

"I bet you nailed them, didn't you?" Bobby said.

"I did pretty well," Tula said.

The doorbell rang. I answered it. It was Toshi.

"Dude, where have you been? The princess is getting mad." He saw Tula and sneered. "Well, look who it is, the Kundabon. That's all she is, Giles. A Kundabon in disguise."

Tula aimed her briefcase at him and sprayed yellow gunk on his face. Toshi fell unconscious. We carried him down into her office, laying him gently on top of her desk. She clicked a button on the side of her desk. It turned into an operating table. She pressed another button, enabling us to look inside Toshi's body, as if his skin was made out of glass. We saw his heart, his ribs, his liver.

Bobby pointed at Toshi's stomach. "Look. He's got an intestinal parasite."

"Bobby's right," Nikki said. "It's a worm."

"No," I said. "It's a caterpillar."

It spun a cocoon near Toshi's pancreas. A second later, a butterfly emerged, the darkest, most malevolent butterfly I've ever seen. It flew between Toshi's ribs and landed on his heart.

"Oh no," Tula said. "The princess planted a black butterfly inside him. If we don't get rid of it he'll be her groupie forever."

"Let's open Toshi's mouth and spray bug spray," Nikki said.

"Your bug spray won't work on a black butterfly, Nikki," Tula said.

"Then how can we kill it?" Bobby asked.

"A black butterfly cannot be killed. It can only be captured."

"How can we capture it?" I said.

"With a black butterfly net. How else?" Tula said.

"Where are we going to get a black butterfly net?" Nikki asked.

"We're going to make one out of a lock of the princess's hair," said Tula.

"A lock of hair? That's voodoo, isn't it?" Bobby said.

"Bobby, voodoo is far more advanced than nuclear science. The dumbest witch doctor on your planet knows twice as much as Einstein ever did."

We climbed out of the briefcase and hurried into Toshi's apartment. Princess Petulance was gone. So were Cable and Heads-or-Tails. I think they were afraid Tula might have them arrested. Juvenile delinquents are scared of the law.

Luckily Toshi's nanny was still out grocery shopping.

"The princess took a ballet class," Tula said. "I bet there's hair all over," she chuckled. Purple girls shed like Saint Bernards.

She was right. The floor was strewn with mint-colored hair. Tula dropped a lock of hair into her briefcase. The briefcase made a loud buzzing sound. When the noise stopped

Tula opened it. A little net with wings came fluttering out. Tula gently opened Toshi's mouth. The net flew inside.

Before you could say "Abracadabrawithpepperoniandextracheese," the net soared back out of his mouth with the butterfly writhing inside it.

"Hooray!" Nikki said.

Tula put the black butterfly in a glass jar, sealed the jar shut and placed it inside her briefcase. "I'll add it to my butterfly collection."

"Why didn't the princess put one inside me, Tula?" I asked.

"Black butterflies are hard to come by, Giles. She's lucky she found one."

Toshi groaned. He was waking up slowly. Or at least he seemed to be. However, ten minutes later he still looked like a zombie.

"Giles, what's something you and Toshi have fun doing together?" Tula asked.

"We love doing play-by-play," I said.

We did it all the time on the school bus. Pretending we both had microphones, we'd do color commentary of an imaginary basketball game between giraffes and zookeepers.

"Do some play-by-play right now," Tula said.

"What good will that do?" I asked.

"It's a kind of magic," Tula said. "On your planet it's called friendship."

I began doing play-by-play. "The point guard is bringing the ball up for the zookeepers. Charging! Offensive foul on the zookeeper. Johnny Giraffe gets two free throws."

Toshi was still a zombie.

"Come on, Toshi," Nikki pleaded. "Snap out of it."

We heard the click of high heel shoes outside the front door.

"It's Toshi's nanny," Bobby said. "What are we going to do?"

"If she sees Toshi like this she'll freak out," I said.

"Keep doing play-by-play, Giles," Tula said, diving into her briefcase.

"Don't leave us," Nikki whispered urgently.

The nanny unlocked the front door.

"Johnny Giraffe is stepping up to the free throw line," I said. "He's shooting eighty-six percent from the line this year. Hey, look at those giraffe cheerleaders. Those sure are some skimpy outfits. You can see practically all their spots."

"Wow," Toshi said, sitting up. "Check out that triple reverse dunk by Jerry Giraffe."

The nanny entered the apartment, lugging three grocery bags.

Toshi smiled at her. "I hope you got peanut butter."

CHAPTER THIRTEEN

(HEY, READER. OK, I screwed up with the whole ballet thing. Mark my words, it won't happen again. What was that? You don't believe me? Thanks for the vote of confidence. Your moral support is greatly appreciated.)

On Thursday morning, four kids and a lawyer hung out inside the briefcase. Nikki and I munched on traffic jam while Tula filled Bobby and Toshi in on what we had to do to transform New York.

"This isn't going to be easy," Bobby said.

"We have three days left to prepare," Tula said. "I want you to think of this as an intergalactic boot camp. You're training to perform a miracle."

"That won't be easy with Grandma snooping around," Nikki said.

"Nikki's right," Bobby said. "How can we possibly pull this off without her finding out?"

"If she finds out, we automatically get evicted," Toshi said.

"Your grandmother's been having trouble sleeping. Isn't that right, Giles?" Tula asked.

"Yes," I said sadly. "Ever since Grandpa died."

"She has insomnia," Bobby said.

"Sleeping pills don't even help," Nikki said.

Reaching into her pocket, Tula pulled out a golden marble. "Tell her to stare at this. It will put her right to sleep. She won't wake up until Monday morning when the test is over."

"Is it safe?" I asked.

"Not only is it safe," Tula said. "It will rejuvenate her. She'll feel thirty years younger."

"We'd better give one to my nanny," Toshi said. "Otherwise, she'll be watching my every move."

Tula gave a golden marble to Toshi too.

He and I climbed out of the briefcase. Toshi took the elevator down to his apartment while I went into Grandma's room.

She was sitting in a chair, staring at the wall. She yawned. The bags under her eyes were so big you could put groceries in them.

"Here, Grandma," I said. "Try this. It's a hypnotic sleeping ball. I got it in a box of cereal."

"Oh, Giles."

"Just give it a shot."

"At this point I'll try anything," she said. It was pretty obvious she didn't think it would work.

"Stare at it," I said.

A minute later, she was snoring. So was Toshi's nanny down on the eighteenth floor.

With the adults out of the way, the entire team gathered in the living room.

"OK," Tula said, popping open her briefcase. "Intergalactic boot camp starts right now."

"There's nothing to worry about," declared Stanley, the parking meter, rolling down a ramp out of the briefcase. "Your hero has arrived."

"Oh no," I muttered under my breath. I yanked Tula into the dining room. "Tula, why did you bring him?"

"He might come in handy, Giles," she said.

"How could a parking meter possibly come in handy?" I asked.

Stanley heard that. He was standing right behind me. "Giles," he said, "are you looking to have a quarter embedded in your forehead?"

"No, Stanley. I . . . I was just kidding. I'm happy to have you. Thank God you're here." I grabbed my little sister, who was walking by chomping on a brownie. "Hey, Nikki, this is Stanley. He's a parking meter. Go take him into your bedroom and play the violin for him."

"What kind of music do you like, Stanley?" Nikki asked.

"I like heavy metal 'cuz that's what I eat. Dimes, quarters, nickels."

"I don't know any heavy metal but I know a nice sonata I think you'll love."

"Bring it on," said Stanley.

They disappeared into her room.

"OK," I said. "At least I got rid of him for a little while."

"Hey, Giles, come in here!" Bobby yelled excitedly from his bedroom.

I rushed down the hallway. Bobby's bedroom had been totally cool-ified.

"This is the command and control center," Tula said, strolling behind me. "It will serve as our dispatch center, our coordination office and our surveillance monitoring center all in one."

All four walls were giant LCD computer screens. So was the ceiling and the floor. There wasn't one square inch of that room that wasn't in high definition. All the streets in

Greenwich Village flashed one by one across one of the walls. Images of Central Park whizzed along the floor beneath us.

"Bobby, you have LCD carpeting," Toshi said, strolling into the room.

"And LCD wallpaper," Bobby added jubilantly.

"Bobby, you can monitor all of Manhattan simultaneously from this room," explained Tula. "You can oversee the multiplication of the droids. You can measure their progress collecting recyclables as they move through the city. You will even be able to follow Giles and Toshi in their flyplanes."

Bobby's desk and chair and ultra-elaborate computer console hovered above us in the middle of the room. "There is only one problem, Tula," he said. "How am I supposed to get up into that chair?"

"By taking a flight of stairs of course." She opened her briefcase.

A set of mahogany stairs with golden wings came fluttering out of the briefcase and soared around the room.

Landing at Bobby's feet, the stairs made a deep hooting sound like an owl on steroids. He climbed them to his computer console and plopped down in the white leather chair. He couldn't stop grinning. "Manhattan," he said, "prepare to become immaculate."

I tried not to get jealous. I knew my gadgets were coming.

Tula snapped her briefcase shut. "Bobby, your primary task is to familiarize yourself with the command and control center." She headed out the door. "Giles, you and Toshi come with me."

She pulled a sign out of her briefcase and stuck it on the kitchen door: FIGHTER PILOT SCHOOL!

"We're a squadron," I said, giving Toshi a high-five.

We entered the kitchen. It looked normal. Nothing was

LCD, not even the cookie jar. Tula directed our attention to a pair of flies sitting on the counter. They were actually miniature spaceships, courtesy of Dr. Sprinkles!

"Each flyplane is equipped with a graffiti-removing laser. Your spaceships are also powerful fighting machines. Princess Petulance is committed to sabotaging this quest, and you must protect the droids. However, your lasers and missiles can only be used in self-defense. And never, under any circumstances, on humans. Do you understand?"

"Got it," I said.

Toshi got it too.

She handed each of us a silver bracelet. "These are your S/Us. They have the power to shrink you down and return you to your normal size. They are encoded with thought-activation software. All you have to do is say to yourself, 'I want to be smaller.' And presto, you'll be tiny."

We slipped on our bracelets.

"You can use your S/U to make somebody else small, too," said Tula. "But an S/U can't make anything larger than its actual size. You can't take a penny and make it the size of the Empire State Building. It's only a shrinking device. Do you understand?"

"No problem," Toshi said.

She picked up one of the flyplanes. "Toshi, this is your flyplane. It's solar powered." She set it down and gently picked up the other one. "Giles, your flyplane runs on rhyming."

"It what?" I said.

"It was custom-made for you by Dr. Sprinkles," she said, setting it back down on the kitchen counter.

I couldn't believe it. "A spaceship that runs on rhyming?"

"It's the first of its kind," Tula said.

"How does it work?" I asked.

"When your flyplane is running low on fuel, it will give you a riddle. You must answer in rhyme. A nonrhyming answer is incorrect."

"How can anything run on rhyming?" asked Toshi.

"Why wouldn't it?" said Tula. "Poetry is the human soul's highest-octane fuel." Her briefcase started blinking. "Looks like I'm due back in court. Good luck, you guys."

She disappeared.

"I guess we should shrink ourselves down," Toshi said, a bit nervous.

"I guess so," I said, trembling a little.

We stared at our flyplanes.

"We should sit on the kitchen counter," Toshi said. "Then we'll be up here by the flyplanes when we're small. Not down on the floor."

"Good point," I said.

We both perched on the edge of the counter. I said to myself, *Make me smaller.*

Suddenly I was standing on the kitchen counter, peering up at the salt shaker as if it was a lighthouse. I'm serious. I was shorter than a blueberry. So was Toshi. When you're shorter than a blueberry, life is good.

The kitchen counter was wider than a football field. If Peyton Manning was my size, he wouldn't have been able to throw a pass to the sink. I peered over the edge of the Formica cliff at the tiled floor down below. Climbing down there would've been like descending Everest.

"I'll race you to the cookie jar," Toshi said.

Huffing and puffing, we pried open the lid and lifted out a chocolate chip cookie, using every muscle in our bodies.

"Let's eat our way through it," I said.

"Fighter pilots need to stock up on carbs," Toshi said, gnawing away.

"Hey, Toshi," I said while chomping, "do you think Tula has a crush on me?"

"I don't know. It's hard to tell with blue girls."

When we were finished gorging, we sipped from a puddle of milk over by the sink and marched to our flyplanes.

Mine had two bulbous eyes, just like a normal fly's. I climbed into the left eye, which contained the pilot's seat. The right eye was the co-pilot's seat. A glass hatch slid down over it like the film over an eye. There was a helmet and goggles lying on the floor by my foot. I put them on and sat down.

Just like when I was valet parking, a silent voice rang out in the center of my brain again.

Hello, Giles. Welcome on board. I am a 2012 miniature star cruiser. I am equipped with thought-activation technology. Let me explain how it works.

I already know how it works. I was driving a star cruiser that had it just the other day.

I was not aware that you had driven a star cruiser, Giles.

Come on. Do you know who you're talking to?

Yes, I'm talking to a warrior poet.

That's me, Giles. What's your name? Do spaceships have names?

Dr. Melissa Sprinkles, the greatest scientist in the entire universe, named me—

Did she program you to say that?

Yes, Giles. As I was saying, Dr. Melissa Sprinkles, the greatest scientist in the entire universe, named me DubDub.

Cool name. OK, let's take off, DubDub.

First I need some fuel.

We need to find a gas station.

Remember, I run on rhyming.

Oh, that's right.

That concerned me. It was one thing to write a little poetry, it was another thing to fuel a spaceship with it.

Giles, if you were put on this planet to eat movie food, what does it mean?

How am I supposed to know, DubDub?

Unfortunately we won't be able to take off until you figure it out, Giles.

Toshi took off in his flyplane. He shot out the kitchen window. Why couldn't I have a solar-powered flyplane?

Tell me the riddle again, DubDub.

If you were put on this planet to eat movie food, what does it mean?

It means you're going to eat a lot of Milk Duds.

Your answer didn't rhyme, Giles. Therefore it is incorrect.

I heard Toshi over my intercom.

"Hey, Giles, where are you? I'm cruising over Central Park."

"I'm having technical difficulties, Toshi."

He laughed. "Dude, your flyplane sucks compared to mine."

I shut off the intercom. I didn't need to hear that right now.

Tell me the riddle again, DubDub.

If you were put on this planet to eat movie food, what does it mean?

I got it. It means you were born to eat popcorn.

Correct, Giles.

We zoomed out the window, over a nasty traffic jam and into Central Park. I met up with Toshi on a dandelion. We rose high above the sycamore trees and flew in formation over the Sheep Meadow, the Bethesda Fountain and the polar bear exhibit in the Central Park Zoo.

"Hey, Toshi," I said into my intercom, "check this out." I landed my flyplane on a gargoyle dangling from a rooftop on Fifth Avenue.

"Watch this," Toshi said, doing a nosedive, landing on a poodle's nose outside the Plaza Hotel.

We flew along Broadway to Times Square, spinning figure eights in the summer sky high above the tourists, then we headed downtown, past the Flatiron Building into Chelsea, the West Village, the Meatpacking District. We were two flyplanes darting with pinpoint accuracy at three hundred miles per hour past hot dog vendors, up fire escapes, around pizza parlor signs.

Imagine the most fun you ever had in your life. Now, multiply that fun by fifty million. That's how much fun it is to go cruising in a flyplane.

We were veering toward South Street Seaport when suddenly a swallow swooped down off a traffic light and started chasing me. Swallows eat flies and this one wanted me, Giles, for lunch.

Toshi circled behind the swallow and shadowed it. "Should I kill it, Giles?"

"No, Toshi. It can't catch me."

"Come on. Let me vaporize it."

"No," I said.

"Tula didn't say we couldn't kill animals."

"Well, I'm saying we can't kill animals. And I'm captain of this team. What I say goes."

"Well, OK," Toshi said.

I shot through SoHo with the bird in hot pursuit. Who would've thought that getting chased by a swallow could be so much fun? Its beak was only inches away. I let it stay close. If we got away too easily, the bird would've been depressed. It would've said to itself, "Boy, I'm the slowest swallow in the whole wide world. I can't even catch a stupid fly."

Swallows get depressed too. I didn't want that. He had no idea he was chasing a star cruiser. By the time we got to Wall Street, he gave up and flew away.

Bobby's image flashed across my console. "Giles, Tula wants you guys to practice removing graffiti over by the West Side Highway."

I followed Toshi to an abandoned building that had graffiti on the walls.

DubDub, do you think Tula would ever go out with me?

I don't know, Giles.

What are you talking about? You're a state-of-the-art

spacecraft. Your main computer knows everything about the known universe.

Love isn't part of the known universe, Giles. It's part of the Great Unknown.

DubDub, I may be a poet but that's still too deep for me.

There was a whole lot of graffiti on this building.

How fast can you remove graffiti, DubDub?

Would you like a demonstration, Giles?

Yes.

It made an entire wall spotless in a fraction of a second.

Not bad, DubDub.

Thank you, Giles.

My smart phone rang in my pocket. And to think, once upon a time this was high-tech.

It was Navida.

"Giles, you still haven't told me your big news."

"My big news?" I said awkwardly. I had already told three kids about the test. That was my limit. I couldn't tell Navida now.

"Yeah," she said, "what's your big news?"

I had to come up with something quick. "Oh. Here it is. Scientists at the Institute for Gluttony invented a new kind of donut."

"You call that big news?"

"Heck, yeah. It's part glaze, part jelly. It's called a glelly donut."

"That's so exciting," she said with zero enthusiasm.

"I thought you'd appreciate it," I said.

"Giles, what are you doing right now to help the environment?"

"It's kind of hard to describe," I said as my flyplane flew upside down past the Empire State Building.

"No, it's not, Giles. Your butt is on a couch and you've got a donut in your mouth."

"I'm not sitting on a couch, Navida."

"Oh, that's right. You're standing on a chair in the kitchen reaching for the glelly donuts your grandma hid on the top shelf."

"I could go for a glelly donut right now, to be honest with you."

"Giles, you're an eco-embarrassment."

"Hey, lay off. I'm trying. Not everyone is smart enough to have a blog like you."

I couldn't make her part of my team but at least I could build up her ego.

"What a joke that is," she said. "My blog sucks."

"Your blog is amazing."

"If it's so amazing then how come no one reads it? I got ten hits last week. Ten hits, Giles. In a city of eight million people, only ten of them read my blog. Is that the most pathetic thing you ever heard or what?"

DubDub glided over Madison Square Garden. "You know what your problem is, Navida?"

"Please tell me. I am dying to know what my problem is."

"People don't know about your blog. What you need is some free advertising."

It was the perfect way to make up for not selecting her for my team. As soon as I got off the phone with her, I consulted with my flyplane.

DubDub, I want every kid in New York to know about Navida's blog. Is there a way to do that?

Absolutely, Giles. Would you like me to do it right now?

Go for it.

Using way beyond nano-technology, DubDub created a cool commercial for Navida's blog faster than a Madison Avenue advertising firm. The eco-mercial opened with a beautiful nature scene that featured a mountain with a waterfall cascading down it. The name of Navida's Web site flashed in bold letters above the waterfall. Then a voice said, "We interrupt our regular programming for an important announcement. Dude, you need to check out Navida's blog. If you don't, you're a complete dweeb."

The commercial was in 3-D. Not just 3-D but Martian 3-D. That meant it didn't require 3-D glasses in order to have the desired effect. Best of all, when the waterfall came spilling out of the screen, the viewer actually got drenched.

Those Martians are quite clever.

My fabulous flyplane broadcast the ad by hacking into every TV signal in Manhattan, focusing exclusively on kid favorites like Nickelodeon, the Disney Channel, MTV. He also hacked into every popular Web site for kids. So basically every kid in New York City who was on a computer or watching TV saw the ad for Navida's blog.

We didn't want parents fainting or drowning, so Dub-Dub programmed the ad in such a way that adult energy would neutralize the 3-D effect. If an adult was watching TV with the child, the ad would appear without it. It wasn't a big issue, since parents hated most of the shows we hacked into, anyway.

The commercial ran at precisely 4:45 in the afternoon. By 4:46, the number of wet kids in New York City increased dramatically. According to what they later posted on Facebook, the kids didn't care if they got grounded for flooding the living room. Getting nailed by that waterfall was funner than going down the Colorado River on a raft.

CHAPTER FOURTEEN

NAVIDA CALLED BACK later that night. "Giles, a miracle happened."

"What do you mean, Navida?" I asked, lounging on my bed after a long day of intergalactic boot camp.

"I just got eighty thousand hits on my blog."

"Sure you did."

"I swear. Eighty thousand hits."

"Are you serious?"

"I am totally serious. Some kid said he saw an ad for my Web site on MTV. Is that crazy or what?"

"Insane," I said.

"How? How did this happen?"

"Well, to tell you the truth, I have a miniature spaceship and I had its main computer hack into all the TV signals in Manhattan."

I knew she wouldn't believe me so it wasn't like I was divulging anything.

"Quit screwing around, Giles. I'm trying to be serious."

"I'm being totally serious, Navida" I said.

"Quit mocking me."

"There's no mocking going on here. The words coming out of my mouth are totally mockless."

"There's no such word as mockless."

"Sarcasmless. Is that a word?"

"It's not a word, Giles. But moron is a word. It's a person too."

"I bet his name begins with the letter *G?*" I said.

"How did you know?"

"OK," I said. "Let's get serious. A miracle occurred. Who cares how? The bottom line is it happened. Deal with it. You're popular."

"Me, popular?" she said. "This is bizarre. It's scary. It's terrifying. It's . . . the greatest thing that ever happened to me!"

That made me feel good. Anytime you can help a girl in a wheelchair, go for it.

I went out into the living room, where Tula and rest of my team were hanging out.

"I can't wait to see these Eco-droids," Toshi said.

"Tula, when is Dr. Sprinkles going to deliver the first one?" I asked. "It's already Thursday night. The test begins in two days."

Tula checked her watch. "Big Daddy should be here in less than an hour."

I was still a little worried that Big Daddy might not show up. What if Dr. Sprinkles was off buying shoes and forgot all about us? How could you trust a lady with a moveable face?

Toshi reached for the traffic jam. "A homeless man saw me removing graffiti in my flyplane this afternoon," he said. "The poor guy fainted. I guess he'd never seen a fly removing graffiti before."

"That could be a big problem," Bobby said. "No one will pay attention to a homeless man. But what if someone else sees us?"

"It'll freak them out," Toshi said.

"They'll call *The New York Times*," I said.

"We need one of those gizmos to make people forget. Like they had in *Men in Black*," Nikki said, strumming a few notes on her violin.

"Nikki, this isn't a movie," Bobby said. "This is real life."

"Yeah," Toshi added. "And in real life droids don't suddenly start multiplying on the streets of Manhattan."

"You're absolutely right," Tula said. "We must devise a way to conceal all abnormal activity." Tula popped open her briefcase. "I've got just the thing."

A rainbow slid out, stretching and stretching until it arched over the living room. It was the brightest band of color New York City had ever seen. Suddenly the rainbow shattered into one hundred pieces. Each piece was alive. Each piece was an alien. They swam through the air, dipping and diving and soaring in unison. They were red, green, yellow, blue, orange, and violet chunks of mist that were shaped like fish.

"They look like fish ghosts," Bobby said, mesmerized.

"What are they, Tula?" Nikki asked.

"They have a rather long name, Nikki," Tula replied. "It would take an hour and a half to pronounce. For the sake of convenience let's call them cloudfish."

(Hey, reader, if you know a word that means infinitely cooler than the word *cool*, please let me know and I'll use it to describe the cloudfish. I'm going to leave an empty space right here   for that word. If anyone can come up with it please text it to me. You can tell all your friends you helped cowrite my Gilesography.)

Bobby burst out laughing. He pointed to the one with the longest whiskers. "Look. It's a catfish cloudfish."

"This guy's a lobster cloudfish," I said pointing to

another. It wasn't really a creature. It was the hint of a creature. I don't know how else to put it.

There were swordfish cloudfish, dolphin cloudfish, manatee cloudfish, an octopus cloudfish. When they merged in midair, they could turn themselves into a giant rainbow, but they could also shed their brightness and turn into a dense gray fog that filled the entire room.

"This is one school of cloudfish," Tula said. "There are five hundred schools hiding out in the clouds above Manhattan. They're all part of our team."

A goldfish cloudfish landed on Toshi's shoulder while two starfish cloudfish balanced themselves on the bow of Nikki's violin.

"Think of them as a living, breathing fog machine," Tula said.

"Mist with an attitude," Toshi said.

"Bobby, you'll be able to mobilize them from your command and control center," explained Tula. "Let's say Giles is removing graffiti from the corner of Second Avenue and Fourteenth Street. You can send a school of cloudfish over there. To any passerby, it will look like a patch of fog."

"No one will see what we're up to."

"Exactly," replied Tula.

The cloudfish communicated by carving letters out of fog. It looked a little like skywriting.

A message appeared out of thin air above the couch: IT IS AN HONOR TO BE PART OF THIS QUEST!

We all cheered.

Three dolphin cloudfish swam laps around my head at supersonic speed. I had to close my eyes to keep from getting dizzy. "Hey, Tula," I said. "Did Dr. Sprinkles invent the cloudfish?"

"No, they come from a planet called Effulgentoria. I represented them in a lawsuit. A neighboring star system was stealing their ozone. We won the case. This is how they're paying me back."

"Now we've got everything we need to clean Manhattan," Bobby said.

"We don't have the Eco-droid yet," I reminded him. "Without the droid we're in big trouble."

Would we all end up in hairy cages because Dr. Sprinkles let us down?

Tula tried to soothe my agitation. She checked her watch. "Big Daddy will be here in less than five minutes. In the meantime . . ." Digging into her briefcase, she handed me a plastic bag full of miniature vending carts. ICE COLD LEMONADE! was printed on the side of each one.

"What are these for?" I asked.

"They're real vending carts that have been shrunken down. By Sunday morning, there will be one thousand androids cleaning the streets of Manhattan. Like all organic beings, they require energy to keep going. They need water and sunlight to digest paper and turn it back into trees, but this process requires a specific kind of water not found on this planet. It'll taste just like lemonade."

"What if a regular person buys the lemonade?" I asked, watching the octopus cloudfish sway its tentacles in rhythm with Nikki's violin.

"Yeah," Toshi said. "There's a heat wave going on. They can't turn people away."

"They won't have to," Tula said. "It has no side effects for humans."

"Which androids will be selling lemonade?" I asked.

"As soon as they're born, fifty androids will automatically

be programmed to serve as street vendors. Each of them will get a cart and serve lemonade to the other Eco-droids."

"Let's just hope we get them," I said.

"You've got me," Stanley said, rolling into the room. "What more do you need?"

"What makes you think we won't get the droids?" Bobby said.

"You haven't met Dr. Sprinkles," I said. "She's not the most reliable scientist in the world."

"Giles," Tula said, "I think you'll want to take that back." She peered inside her briefcase. "Here comes Big Daddy."

We clapped madly, hooting and hollering. Cloudfish are awesome and so are flyplanes. But an android that can create an entire army of Eco-droids simply by picking up bottles and cans off the street? An android programmed with environmental-reversal software that can turn paper back into trees? Now, that's the most awesomely awesomest thing in the history of awesomeness.

We went berserk with excitement, jumping up and down, making the hardwood floor shake. We all fell silent when Tula rose slowly off the couch and moved into the middle of the living room.

A red carpet spilled out of the briefcase onto the floor as my lovely blue lawyer announced, "Everyone, say hi to Big Daddy."

The android climbed out of the briefcase and walked into our lives. With a name like Big Daddy, I half expected a yeti. But he was a shrimp like me. And he looked completely harmless. He looked like a tiny, bald, middle-aged white guy who fixes computers.

But at least he made it. Dr. Sprinkles was a lady—I mean a blob—of her word.

Nikki ran down the red carpet and gave him a hug. "Welcome, Big Daddy."

He wore blue overalls. "Big Daddy is pleased to be here," he said in a squeaky nerdy voice. He made eye contact with me. "You can call me Big Daddy." He walked over by Toshi. "You too can call me Big Daddy." He shook hands with Bobby. "I go by the name of Big Daddy." He gazed up at a catfish cloudfish. "Hey, you. Please refer to me at all times as Big Daddy."

"OK, OK," said the parking meter. "We get it. You're Big Daddy. Say it one more time I'm spitting a quarter at you."

The android marched right up to Stanley. "Let me give you some advice. Never talk like that to Big Daddy."

The only thing that wasn't geeky about Big Daddy was the way he breathed, deep and long. It wasn't scary like Darth Vadar. Just strange.

"Boy, he sure is a heavy breather," Toshi said.

"He's cleaning the air," Tula said. "The Eco-droids are equipped with air purifiers. By the end of the day the air quality in Manhattan will improve by three hundred percent. Just as the judge requested, you will return Manhattan to its original splendor and prove, beyond the shadow of a doubt, that your species is capable of taking care of the planet."

The doorbell rang. Tula dove into her briefcase. Stanley rolled in behind her.

Bobby answered the front door. It was Buck's dad the building superintendent.

"What's up with all that racket?" he growled. "I've been getting complaints. You've been screaming like maniacs and jumping up and down. The people below you can hear everything."

"Sorry, sir. It won't happen again," Bobby assured him.

"Why aren't you kids in bed?" asked the super.

"We're having a sleepover," Nikki said.

"A sleepover? With who? A herd of rhinos?"

"Have you ever had a pillow fight with a rhino, sir?" I said. "It's a lot of fun."

"Don't get smart with me. Let me talk to your grandmother."

"She's sleeping," I said.

He rolled his eyes. "No adult supervision. Just like I thought."

"There's an adult here," Nikki said, resting her head in the android's lap. "His name is Big Daddy."

"He's our uncle," I said.

The nerdy android stood up and moved toward the door.

The super towered over him. "You're Big Daddy?"

"I dare you to call me Little Daddy. Go ahead. I dare you."

In order not to be noticed, the cloudfish had turned themselves into a rainbow.

"Why is there a rainbow in your living room?" asked the super.

Nikki smiled. "We're happy people."

"If I hear one more peep out of you I'm calling the cops." He marched out the door.

Toshi and I shrank everyone down with our S/Us so the super couldn't hear us. You can scream all you want when you're only an inch tall.

"Even though I'm an inch tall I'm still Big Daddy," squeaked the android.

"Giles, what's wrong?" Tula said, noticing the dazed look on my face.

"First I get a talking parking meter," I said. "Now I have

to deal with this crazy droid. Will the rest of the droids blab like him?"

"No. He's the master droid. Dr. Sprinkles gave him a colorful personality just for the heck of it. His offspring will be much calmer."

"I hope so," I said.

"Giles, you seem stressed out to me. You need to take a little break." She led me toward the flyplane. "Want to take a ride in DubDub?"

Me and Tula all alone! This was the opportunity I'd been waiting for. We zoomed out the window together. Cruising through Central Park in the flyplane was more romantic than a horse-and-buggy ride under a full moon.

I tried to think of something funny to say. When you're alone with a cute girl it's important not to be boring.

"Hey, Tula, where do cloudfish keep their money?"

"I don't know, Giles. Where do cloudfish keep their money?"

"In a fog bank. Get it?"

She gave me a big stupid grin. A big stupid grin isn't really stupid. No way. It's the most precious kind of smile a girl can give you. It's an "I've got a crush on you" kind of smile.

"Hey, Tula, what's it like to walk across a Bridgeling?"

"It feels like you're traveling across eternity, yet you're only taking a few steps."

"Do you think someday I could walk across one?"

"I don't know, Giles. We'd have to get the judge's approval first."

"If we pass the test, do you think he'd give me the green light?"

"Possibly," she said.

In the park down below, someone was blasting a boom-box.

"Do you know what would be a cool name for a band?" I said. "The Chocolate-Covered Rats."

"I'd buy their CD," Tula said.

"I think that's what I'll be when I grow up," I said. "A professional rock band namer."

I could tell Tula was impressed that I was already starting to think about my career. The silhouette of an oak tree loomed up ahead in the moonlight. I decided to show off a little more.

"See that oak tree?" I said. "When the wind passes through it, it makes a certain sound. And the sycamore makes a completely different sound. Every tree has a different voice. Not many people on this planet know that."

Passionately committed to impressing the girl with cotton candy hair, I silently commanded DubDub to zip down into a hole at the base of a poplar tree. Everything went pitch-black.

"Where are we, Giles?" she asked.

DubDub activated the night-vision capability. We were sitting on the nose of a baby raccoon. He was wrestling with his sister while his mama raccoon lay curled up in a ball, fast asleep. The flyplane darted back and forth from one baby's bandit face to the other's long fluffy tail.

Because we were so small, the raccoon's den seemed like a sprawling cave.

"Giles, what was that noise?" Tula asked.

A soft whimpering sound emanated from the back of the den.

"Let's go check it out," I said.

We found a third baby off by itself. It looked sick. It was

smaller and paler, with watery eyes. It lay on its side, showing its belly, which was covered with fleas.

"How dare they suck that poor raccoon's blood?" said Tula.

"Don't worry," I said. "I'll take care of it."

Even I sort of wanted to blast them with a laser but I remembered that I never killed things—no matter what great gizmos I had—so I sprayed them with an insect repellant. The fleas fled for their lives, shocked that a housefly was bombarding them. DubDub translated the flea noises into English. They were screaming, "Traitor!"

Using the flyplane, I applied an antibiotic ointment to the baby raccoon's cuts and soared out of the cavernous den into the moonlight sky.

Tula couldn't take her eyes off me. "You're so connected to nature, Giles. That's what I love about you."

She just said the word *love* and the word *Giles* in the same sentence!

She reached over and took hold of my hand. How soft they were, her lovely little sky fingers.

We flew home and landed in the kitchen. I helped her out of the flyplane. Just as we were about to return to our normal size, a rhyme popped into my head. "I just came up with a poem about tonight. Wanna hear it?"

"Sure."

"I can't," I said. "I'm embarrassed."

"Giles, please."

"Forget I ever mentioned it."

"Giles . . ."

"OK. OK." I was already blushing and I hadn't even recited it yet. If you sucked the red out of every strawberry on earth and squeezed it onto my face, that's about how red I looked. I cleared my throat.

> *"I may only be eleven*
> *but I've already been to heaven*
> *the night I held your hand."*

When blue girls blush their cheeks turn orange. I had a tangerine lawyer.

"Giles, that's the most beautiful thing anyone's ever said to me. But . . ."

"But what?"

"But aren't you thirteen?"

"Yes. But heaven doesn't rhyme with thirteen."

She grinned. "I love it. Could you write it down for me? I'll keep it for the rest of my life."

CHAPTER FIFTEEN

I'VE GOT A GIRLFRIEND!
I've got a girlfriend!
I've got a girlfriend!

SIXTEEN

CHAPTER **SIXTEEN**

HEY, DUDE, GUESS WHAT?
  I've got a girlfriend!

CHAPTER **SEVENTEEN**

I CHANGED MY RELATIONSHIP status on Facebook. No more of that single garbage. I didn't mention that I was dating an alien, though.

On Friday morning, my dad posted a photograph of an orangutan on my Wall, an orangutan coming out of the jungle. (Remember reader—all this time they've been away. They don't know what they've been missing.)

I called him in Malaysia. He answered on the third ring.

"Hi, Dad."

"Hello, Giles. How's it going?"

"Just another boring summer vacation. How's it going with you?"

"It's great. Did you check your Facebook?"

"Heck, yeah. How close was the orangutan, Dad?"

"Real close, son."

"How big was it?"

"A lot bigger than I thought."

"Did it say anything?"

"As a matter of fact it did. It asked me if I had any cookie dough."

"What did you say?"

"I said I had a bunch, but my son Giles ate it all."

"So now the orangutan hates my guts. Thanks, Dad."

"Not at all. I told him you're a nature boy. He decided to cut you some slack."

"I love it when orangutans cut me slack."

My dad and I could banter like this for hours. People say I inherited his wacky imagination.

"Where's Mom?" I asked.

"Up in a tree picking coconuts. You know your mom. She loves coconuts."

My mom grabbed the phone from my dad and said, "I do love coconuts, Giles. But I love throwing them at your father even more."

My parents loved teasing each other almost as much as they loved teasing me. How would they feel about me dating a blue girl? I guess they didn't notice my relationship status on Facebook. Hopefully it wouldn't freak them out. Blue was my mom's favorite color. That had to count for something, didn't it?

"How's Grandma?" my mother asked. Grandma was my mom's mom.

"She's sleeping," I said.

My mother was stunned. "You mean she actually fell asleep?"

"Yeah, Mom. Grandma's in a deep sleep."

"Oh, I'm so happy to hear that," my mother said. "That's the best news I've heard all week."

Then Nikki and Bobby got to talk to Mom and Dad, too.

Later that afternoon, Toshi and I flew our flyplanes down into the subways to become acclimated to subterranean conditions. (Hey reader, how do you like the words acclimated and subterranean? Get out your dictionary, dude!) I didn't tell

Toshi about my date with Tula. I tried to stay focused. After all, this was boot camp, not the latest episode of *The Bachelor*.

When we got back around four, I broke down and told Stanley all about my date with Tula. I had to tell someone.

He was happy for me but a moment later his voice turned glum.

"I'll never have a girlfriend," he said.

"Yes, you will."

"Who would want to go out with a parking meter?"

"I don't know," I said. "A steak knife maybe."

"I'm not attractive to steak knives."

"What about a cell phone?" I said. "I'll introduce you to mine."

"I hate your ring tone."

"I'll change it."

"What's the point? No one could ever be attracted to me."

Stanley's sadness must've been contagious because a miserable thought rattled around inside my brain. If we failed the test and got evicted, would Tula be allowed to visit me on Desoleen? I had a horrible feeling the answer was no. Would I be allowed to see my parents on Desoleen? Maybe not. Maybe all families would be separated, all the kids herded into one camp and all the adults in another. The two camps would be separated by a towering barbed-wire fence and guarded over by Kundabons.

With no adult supervision, we kids would never have to go to school again. But even that wouldn't be any fun. Not on Desoleen it wouldn't.

I couldn't allow that to happen. We had to prove to the judge that we were capable of stewarding the planet.

Wait a minute. I still didn't know what *stewarding* really meant.

Even with Big Daddy and the cloudfish and the fly-planes, could we possibly clean Manhattan in one day? I had a hard time believing we could.

Stanley and I stood side by side in the kitchen, equally depressed. I pretended to sweep the floor around us.

"What are you doing?" he asked.

"I'm sweeping with my gloom broom, Stanley."

"What's a gloom broom?"

"It sweeps away sadness. Grandpa invented it. Whenever anyone was sad, he'd pull out an imaginary broom and start sweeping with it."

"That's the dumbest thing I ever heard," Stanley said.

"If it's so stupid then why are you laughing?" I asked.

He wasn't the only one cracking up. So was I. That's how the gloom broom worked. People thought it was so stupid they couldn't help laughing. Then their sadness disappeared. That was the secret of the gloom broom.

In a much better mood, I popped into Grandma's room and swept all around her bed in case she was having a bad dream. I didn't think she was because she had a sweet smile on her face.

Her trash basket was full. I picked it up and dumped it down the trash chute outside our apartment. Before I could get back through the door, Buck had me cornered. He grabbed the trash can and smashed it over my head. "Where's your lion, Giles? I thought you were going to feed me to the lions."

I marched into my bedroom, plotting my revenge. After all, I was a superhero. You don't pick on a superhero and get away with it. I had an obligation to the superhero community. I didn't want to get stripped of my superhero privileges.

So I shrank myself and climbed in the flyplane.

DubDub, if I wanted to borrow a lion from the Central Park Zoo for an hour or two, could we do it?

It could be done, Giles. However, I have a hard time understanding the need for a lion at this particular moment.

You'll see. I'll be right back, DubDub.

I hopped out of the cockpit and made myself big again. Despite being a superhero, I didn't feel like being alone in the spaceship with a lion, so I tracked down the parking meter in the kitchen. "I need you, Stanley."

"Finally someone needs me!"

I miniaturized the two of us and strapped him into the copilot's seat. We flew over to the zoo and glided between the iron bars into the lion's cage.

DubDub fired a tranquilizer dart into the lion's leg. It didn't put him to sleep like a normal tranquilizer. Instead, it made the lion friendly and cuddly. I shrank it down and looped a leash around its neck. It licked my face while I tied the end of the leash around Stanley in the copilot's seat.

Stanley trembled. Quarters jingled inside him. "Do lions eat parking meters?" he asked.

"No."

"Are you sure?"

"Yes, I'm sure."

As we were leaving Central Park, the flyplane sputtered and did a nosedive.

Stanley panicked. "What's wrong?"

"Relax, Stanley," I said, landing the spaceship on an empty park bench in the dark. "We need to fuel up."

DubDub gave me a riddle.

Small silver armored creatures are embroidered on my bed sheets, Giles. What do I have?

That's easy, DubDub. You've got armadillos on your pillows.

The gas gauge shot back up to FULL. We cruised back home: me, Stanley and the purring lion.

DubDub flew silently through Buck's bedroom window. Buck was fast asleep, snoring.

Using the S/U, I made me and my new furry friend big again. I crept over to the bed and tickled Buck's foot. He woke up, saw me holding a lion on a leash.

"Look, Buck. I got him at Macy's."

Buck almost wet his bed.

"He was on sale, Buck," I said.

Tears ran down Buck's bully face.

"Ten percent off. Plus I had a coupon."

Buck ran out of the room screaming.

I shrank the two of us back down, rode on the lion's back over to the flyplane and waited.

I heard Buck yell, "THERE'S A LION IN MY BED-ROOM! THERE'S A LION IN MY BEDROOM!"

His dad threw open the door, took one look inside and walked away, yawning. "You were having a nightmare, moron."

Buck peered into his room, saw that it was empty, and climbed back into bed.

Perched invisibly on the windowsill, I turned on the

flyplane's loudspeaker and said, "Hey, Buck, you weren't dreaming!"

I let the lion roar over the loudspeaker. Buck ran out of the room again, hysterical.

(Hey, reader, I have a confession to make. I just love being me, Giles.)

I brought the lion back to the zoo. When I zapped it with the S/U, its body became big but its head only partially expanded to the size of a cat's head. It looked like something out of a freak show.

DubDub, what happened to the lion?

I think it has something to do with the S/U, Giles. It's malfunctioning.

I can't leave it like this. They can't have a lion with a cat's head in the Central Park Zoo. It would give the zoo a bad reputation.

I miniaturized the lion and brought it back to the apartment to show Tula.

Tula wasn't thrilled about it. Not one bit. "Giles, what does a lion have to do with cleaning Manhattan?"

"Nothing."

"What does Buck have to do with it?"

"Buck is an idiot," I said. "He deserved to get nailed."

"I told you, Giles," Tula said, gripping her briefcase like a weapon. A boyfriend pulverizer. "This technology cannot be used against humans."

"It was a practical joke," I explained. "It didn't hurt anybody."

"Well, the lion doesn't seem to be in very good shape," Tula said.

"We can fix it, can't we?"

She didn't answer.

"Can't we, Tula? Don't tell me I hurt the lion. Lions have it bad enough on this planet. Their jungles and savannas keep getting turned into mini-malls."

Nikki fed the little-headed lion her ice cream cone. "I think he's cute," she said. "I say we keep him like this."

"It wasn't my fault, Tula," I said. "My S/U malfunctioned." I removed it from my wrist and handed it to her.

She dropped it into her briefcase, pulled it out a second later. "There. It's fixed. There was a loose wire."

I slid it back on and shrank the lion. When I made it big again, the body and the head returned to their normal size. The evenly proportioned lion gave off a deep purr.

Big Daddy stroked his mane. "You may be the king of beasts but I'm Big Daddy."

Tula didn't pet the lion. Instead, she glared at me. I'd never seen her so mad. She was fuming. "You're losing focus, Giles. When I get distracted we end up in a chicken coop. If you get distracted you'll end up on Desoleen. That's a million times worse than a chicken coop."

She had a point there. My girlfriend was losing faith in me. Man, did that ever suck.

I returned the lion to its cage at the zoo. Its filthy cage looked like a loft in SoHo compared to the one I would soon be stuffed into. My cage would have a big hairy wart on it.

I flew back home, the world's most pathetic superhero, a kid who'd rather play a prank on a bully than save the planet.

Navida called late Friday night. I was tempted to let it go straight to voice mail but I didn't. Kids typically don't pick up when a girl in a wheelchair is calling. Navida was used to it. She got that all the time.

"What's up, Navida?" I said.

"Giles, I've got a big problem."

"Not as big as the one I've got. I can promise you that."

"Giles, I can't think of anything to put in my blog. I've got writer's block. No, worse than that. I've got blog block. I've got major blog block, Giles. Eighty thousand kids are waiting for me to write something. The pressure is getting to me. Help!"

"OK," I said slowly. "Here's what you should write. 'If we only had one day to prove that we actually cared about the earth, what would you do to make a difference?'"

"That's a great idea, Giles."

"Let's say that day was this Sunday. What would you do?"

"I love it. I'm using it. But tell me this. What happens if we're unable to prove that we care about the earth?"

"I don't know," I said. "Something really bad."

I felt like I was sinking into quicksand, mouth first.

"But this is all hypothetical, Navida." I emphasized the word *hypothetical*. "There's no way we're about to get kicked off the planet. It's pure make-believe. It's really important that you understand this, Navida. What I'm saying isn't real."

"I get it. I get it," she said. "But it's still brilliant. Thank you, Giles. You just wrote my blog for me."

When I hung up, Tula was standing by my computer. I didn't even hear her enter the room.

"That was Navida," I said, guilt ridden.

"I know, Giles."

"I screwed up again, didn't I? I wasn't supposed to tell her anything. Face it, Tula. I'm a complete failure."

"No, you're not."

"I'm not?"

"I'm glad you told Navida."

"But I was only allowed to tell three kids."

"You didn't break the law for one simple reason. You told her it was purely hypothetical."

"I did emphasize the word *hypothetical*."

"Without revealing the threat of eviction, you figured out a way to get her involved. You made her an unofficial member of the team."

"And you're OK with that?"

"Giles, you did the right thing."

"I did the right thing. Oh my God. How bizarre."

She smiled. Nothing feels better than making your girlfriend smile, especially when you have a nasty habit of making her sad.

CHAPTER EIGHTEEN

"**GUESS WHAT, GILES?**" Navida said. "Your blog idea was a huge success. Tons of kids are planning to do stuff tomorrow to prove they care about the planet. I'm helping them get organized."

"What kind of stuff are you doing?" I asked, holding the phone in one hand, while stepping over (but not picking up) piles of dirty clothes in my room.

"Well, starting at nine in the morning, we're all preparing a litterless breakfast. At nine thirty we're going through our apartments unplugging unused electronic devices. They waste electricity even when they're turned off. At ten we're turning up the thermostats on our air conditioners two degrees and making sure every light in the house has a compact fluorescent bulb. At ten fifteen we're all writing letters on the Internet to the governor asking for more wind and solar power. That's just the small stuff. Wait until we get rolling."

"That sounds good," I said. "Just don't get in my way. I've got an entire city to clean."

"Giles, quit acting like a superhero."

"I'm not acting, Navida." I'd been impersonating one my entire life. Those days were over.

I wished Navida good luck and went into the kitchen. It

was Saturday afternoon. The test would begin in nine hours. I tried to stay calm but it wasn't easy. I was the only one who'd been to Desoleen, the only one who'd actually seen a Kundabon. Nikki, Bobby and Toshi had no idea what was in store for us if we failed. They were upbeat and joking at lunch. Not me.

"Where's my traffic jam?" Toshi said. "It was right here."

"I guess it drove away," Nikki said.

Toshi chomped on a bagel. "No, Nikki. I think you ate it."

"Did not."

"Oh no? Then open your mouth."

Nikki reluctantly opened her mouth. A voice could be heard all the way down in her stomach. "Hey, don't drive in the fast lane if you're only going fifty-five!"

"Right, you didn't eat it," Toshi said.

Ten cloudfish formed a protective wall around Nikki. She seemed to have a magic power over them. I don't know if it was her violin playing or what. They loved her.

Tula appeared out of thin air. "I'm sorry I'm late. I had urgent business."

I always felt a billion times better when the girl with the cotton candy hair was in the room.

Toshi peanut-buttered a slice of bread and handed it to her. "Tula, I get it that Giles and I are supposed to get rid of all the graffiti." He hesitated. "It's just that not all graffiti is bad."

"What are you talking about, Toshi?" Bobby said. "Graffiti is disgusting." Bobby and I had been getting along OK, but this was his usual goodie-goodie self showing through.

"Murals aren't," Toshi said. "Murals are cool."

"Don't worry, Toshi," Tula said. "Your flyplanes are equipped with art critic software. They will not erase murals."

"Now that we're on the subject. Something's been bothering me too" I said, dragging my spoon through a bowl of Rice Krispies.

"What is it, Giles?" asked Tula.

"There are a lot of animals in this city that live off trash. Mice, rats, squirrels, pigeons. What will happen to them when we clean up Manhattan?"

"They'll starve to death," Bobby said happily.

"I have a problem with that," I said.

"Giles, I think the S/U permanently shrunk your brain," Bobby said.

The insult didn't bother me. It's amazing what doesn't bother you when you finally have a girlfriend.

Bobby grabbed a blueberry out of a bowl and flung it at me. "This bozo feeds ants. Can you believe it? He feeds ants."

"I suppose you step on them," said Big Daddy.

"You're darn right I do," Bobby said.

The cloudfish wrote a message overhead: BOBBY'S A LOSER!

"I happen to be number one in my class," Bobby said.

They wrote another message: YOU'RE STILL A LOSER!

I'd never seen Bobby so mad. The words that came out of Tula's mouth made him even madder.

"Giles is right, Bobby. Manhattan has a delicate ecosystem. The elimination of mice will have a devastating effect on the cat population."

"Do not worry," said Big Daddy. "My children will not pick up food. Only plastics and glass and paper and paper byproducts. We just want recyclables." He walked over to the kitchen window and looked down at the city. "If someone drops a Big Mac on the street, my children will not pick it up. The mice and the rats and the ants and the squirrels and the pigeons and the crows and the seagulls will take care of it. That's their job. What we're going after is the wrapper. This we can turn back into trees. We cannot take a Big Mac and turn it back into a cow."

"Dr. Sprinkles is working on that," Tula said.

Nikki melted some butter in the microwave and poured it on Stanley's bowl of quarters.

"Thank you, Nikki," Stanley said.

"What about the homeless?" I said. "They collect bottles and cans for money. We're taking away their source of income."

"I can't believe I'm hearing this," Bobby said, jumping up from the table, pacing furiously back and forth. "If we get evicted our entire species will be homeless."

"Are you sure you're number one in your class?" asked Big Daddy.

"Why is everyone picking on me?" Bobby yelled.

BECAUSE YOU'RE A LOSER! wrote the cloudfish.

Bobby stormed out of the room. I can't say I didn't enjoy it.

"Giles, don't worry about the homeless," Toshi said. "They'll only be without bottles and cans for one day. The city will go back to its filthy old ways on Monday."

"It better not," Tula said. "Or your species will be in big trouble."

"This quest will be a blessing for the homeless, Giles," Big Daddy said. "When my children clean the streets they'll find money and jewelry people have accidentally dropped. We'll give it to the homeless."

"Why can't we keep it?" Toshi asked.

"Kindness first," Tula said. "Always at all times. Always."

"That's our motto," I said.

Tula gave me a big, stupid grin. If I got stranded in a desert, I'd rather have a big, stupid grin than a canteen full of water. I could live off it for months.

I went to see Bobby in command and control. For the first time in my life I felt bad that he was getting picked on.

"The cloudfish pick on everyone, Bobby. Not just you," I said. "Look. They're even teasing the flight of stairs."

Two dolphin cloudfish chased the flight of stairs around the room. It took me a couple of minutes to shoo the frisky cloudfish out into the living room.

Finally able to feel safe, the flight of stairs fluttered down to the ground, chirping merrily. Bobby tossed it some breadcrumbs and climbed up to his computer console. I followed him. All the buttons and gauges and flickering lights on a spaceship were nothing compared to what Bobby had on his console.

"Have you figured out how to work all these gadgets?" I said.

"Of course I have," he said.

I knew he'd say that. I wanted him to. We couldn't afford to have him moping. He was an integral part of the team.

"Just watch this." Bobby pressed a button.

"What is it?"

"Not only can I see all of New York on these screens," Bobby bragged. "I can see the entire universe."

A baby crib appeared on one of the wall screens, floating in deep space. It terrified me. You're probably wondering how a baby crib could freak someone out. Well, this crib was one thousand miles long. The bars on the crib were made out of boiling bloodred mist. The entire thing rested on four giant pillars of black fog that crackled with lightning. Only

Kundabons could hatch in a place like that. There must've been thousands of them inside that colossal crib.

Bobby twirled a knob on his console, giving us a glimpse inside the crib. What we discovered weren't a bunch of baby Kundabons. The crib contained half a dozen massive discs of blinding light.

"What are they?" I said.

"Baby stars," Bobby replied.

"Baby what?"

"The universe is expanding, Giles. New stars are being born every day. They have to go somewhere. So they built the Stellar Nursery."

The stars cuddled together under sheets of flame and burning blankets of cosmic dust. Whizzing all around them were gale force winds.

"Baby stars love chaos, Giles. They couldn't live without it."

"If you think that's cool," I said, "you should see the Bridgelings."

"What's a Bridgeling?" he asked.

I told him.

"Wait," he said. "You mean they're alive?"

He commanded his computer to track them down. The Bridgelings didn't appear on any of the giant screens, though.

"I don't get it," Bobby said. "I have access to the entire cosmos."

"Bridgelings are very mysterious. It doesn't surprise me, Bobby."

He tried to track down the Halls of Universal Justice. It didn't show up either.

"I bet it has an invisibility shield," I said.

His eyes bulged with wonder when I described the Pollen-doozees and the crystalline judge. It was fun hanging out with Bobby. It reminded me of the old days, when we'd built a tree fort together deep in the heart of the woods.

He pressed another button on the console. "Look what I found on Intergalactic YouTube."

"There's an Intergalactic YouTube?" I asked.

"Of course there is," he said.

Princess Petulance flashed across the floor screen.

"She must have her own Web cam," Bobby said. "She's constantly posting stuff."

In the video clip she was parading through a palace, completely ignoring the fact that pillars were crumbling and tapestries on the wall were on fire and someone was hurling a rock through a stained-glass window. None of that bothered the princess in the least.

Her mom and dad rushed over to her.

"Young lady, where do you think you're going?" hissed the queen.

"Disco dancing. There's a rave. The Witches of Never-ending Misery are throwing it. Lousy dancers get dumped into their cauldron. It's amazing."

"You can't go disco dancing," insisted the queen.

"Why not?"

"Because we're under attack!" bellowed the king, who was clutching a laser gun awkwardly in his purple hands, trying to figure out how it worked.

"The rebels want to chop off our heads," shrieked the queen.

"They blame us for draining our planet of all its natural resources," said the king.

"There's nothing I hate more than rebel scum who believe in truth and justice," said the princess. "Especially when they keep me from going to a rave."

Her tattoo pirate fired a little cannon out the window.

"Good shot," said the princess.

The pirate saluted her.

The screen went blank.

"She wants to turn Central Park into a mall, Bobby," I told him. "That means good-bye to the Sheep Meadow and Strawberry Fields."

"Well, it won't be happening," Bobby said. "'Cuz we're not getting evicted."

"What if she tries to sabotage us?"

"I'm not scared of her."

"You think we'll succeed in our quest?" I asked.

"Of course we will," Bobby said.

Our quest. That was the first time I ever thought of it as our quest, not my quest. That was a mature way of looking at it. That was highly unusual for me, Giles.

Following Bobby into the living room, I wondered how many mature thoughts you had to have each day in order to be considered an adult. Ten? Fifteen? What's the cutoff for being an adult? Could you still do stupid kid stuff as long as you met your quota of mature thoughts each day?

"I hope you guys are ready," Tula said. "The test starts in seven hours."

"You're darn right we're ready," Toshi said. "Aren't we, Giles?"

"Heck, yeah," I said. "Aren't we, Bobby?"

"Absolutely," my brother said. "What about you, Big Daddy? Are you ready?"

"Big Daddy is always ready," replied the android.

"Isn't someone going to ask me if I'm ready?" asked Stanley.

"Are you ready, Stanley?" Toshi said.

"I'll spit quarters at Princess Petulance if she tries to interfere," said the parking meter.

The only unenthusiastic member of our team was Nikki. She looked miserable.

"What's wrong, Nikki?" I said.

"I don't have a job," Nikki said. "Everyone has something cool to do except me." A tear slid down her cheek. "Being a little girl sucks."

"Little girls rock," Tula said. "That's why I'm giving you the most important job of all."

"You are?" Nikki said.

Tula opened her briefcase and handed a set of papers to Nikki. "Can you read this sheet music, Nikki?"

"Yes. What is it?"

"It's a violin solo for a very special symphony called *The Music of the Spheres*."

"Never heard of it," Nikki said glumly.

"It's a symphony of magic," Tula said.

Nikki's mouth dropped wide-open. "Magic?"

"Nikki, an ordinary symphony has a beginning and an end. *The Music of the Spheres* is eternal."

"An eternal symphony? Don't the musicians ever get tired?" Nikki asked.

"Never," Tula said. "It is the sound of peace and harmony in its purest form. Other noises try to drown it out. Sometimes they succeed. Sometimes the musicians need a little help. You've been chosen to play a solo, Nikki." Tula put her sky blue arm around the six-year-old. "Tonight at midnight it will begin. It will last for seven minutes. You will repeat the solo at the beginning of every hour for twenty-four hours, until the test ends on Sunday at midnight. The melody of universal peace will restore harmony between humankind and Planet Earth."

A starfish cloudfish balanced itself on the tip of Nikki's violin bow like a star on a Christmas tree.

"You will be hooked up to a microphone, Nikki," Tula said. "When the Eco-droids go through the city cleaning, each one will be equipped with an iPod. They'll be listening to your solo. They need your music as much as they require sunlight and lemonade. They won't accomplish anything without the enchanting sound of your violin."

Big Daddy whipped out his iPod. "Big Daddy listens only to you, Nikki," the android promised. "He could care less about Lady GaGa."

"Without *The Music of the Spheres* this city cannot be transformed," Tula said. "It's the final ingredient, Nikki. You are the final ingredient."

"I'm so important!" Nikki declared.

"Nikki, you'll be playing alongside the largest orchestra in the cosmos," Tula said. "It is the cosmos."

"Are you saying the cosmos is one giant orchestra, Tula?" Toshi asked.

"Everything is music," she said, tapping her fingers on her briefcase. "Planets, stars, comets, asteroids . . ."

"This is better than traffic jam!" Nikki shouted. She popped a little red truck in her mouth. "Almost." She ran off with the sheet music. "I'd better start practicing right now." She stopped in the doorway and turned around. "Tula, why'd you wait so long to give it to me?"

"I apologize, Nikki. I've been waiting for that sheet music since Wednesday. The judge finally approved it."

"Don't worry," I said. "My little sister can memorize a solo like that in half an hour. She's a prodigy."

Bobby stood up. He had the most serious expression I've ever seen on his face. "Everything is in place. We're ready to clean Manhattan."

I got up and entered Grandma's bedroom quietly. I held her hand for a long time. I must've dozed off for a bit because Tula was tapping me on the shoulder and whispering, "Giles, it's eleven forty-five. The test begins in fifteen minutes."

I kissed Grandma gently on the cheek and whispered, "Wish us luck, Grandma." I straightened her blanket. I tucked her in. "When you wake up, this city will look so different you won't even recognize it."

I met up with Toshi in the kitchen. We shrank down and climbed in our flyplanes. I slipped on my helmet and goggles.

Are you ready, DubDub?

I'm ready, Giles!

The clock struck twelve.

Tula thundered, "LET THE TEST BEGIN!"

Toshi and I gave each other the thumbs-up sign. We soared out the window into the night, followed by an army of cloudfish.

CHAPTER **NINETEEN**

NEW YORK IN JULY, you gotta have AC. I had it blasting while I kicked back in the cockpit, calm and cool and comfortable, doing laser removal of swear words spray-painted on walls and doors. In half an hour I cleaned off all the graffiti on the Upper West Side while the cloudfish did their thing, creating patches of fog that fooled thousands of people.

Toshi and I were graffiti hunters roaming the streets of Spanish Harlem, zeroing in on walls and doors that had been tagged.

"Hey, Giles," Toshi said over my intercom at one in the morning, "not only do we get to save the world, we get to stay up all night!"

"I know," I said. "I'm not even tired."

"Neither am I."

When you embark on a quest, you get a burst of energy that never stops bursting.

Toshi called his flyplane Superfly. "Hey, Giles," he said, "I bet Superfly can clean One Hundred Tenth Street faster than DubDub can clean Riverside Drive."

"It's a bet," I said.

While I zapped graffiti off a row of brownstones, Bobby kept me up-to-date on how the rest of the cleaning process was going, feeding me images that streamed across the monitor mounted above my control panel.

Androids were reproducing all over town, in alleys and doorways, on subway platforms, multiplying in the mist. By four in the morning one thousand androids, resembling both men and women, were cleaning the streets of Manhattan. Some were black, some white, others looked Pakistani, Japanese. Some were tall, others puny like Big Daddy. They all wore blue overalls with big red letters printed on back. The letters varied from droid to droid, depending on what neighborhood they were assigned to. Some said, READY, WILLING & ABLE or VILLAGE CLEANING ALLIANCE or EAST MIDTOWN CLEAN PATROL or MANHATTAN GLEAM TEAM.

They blew my mind, these creatures made out of crumpled soda cans, these heroes made out of hot-dog wrappers marching through Hell's Kitchen.

The trash that littered the sidewalks wasn't trash talking anymore. It was terrified.

Bobby sent me a video clip of an android handing a diamond ring to a homeless man. "*I found this. You can have it.*"

"*Thanks, dude.*" The homeless man darted into an all-night pawnshop.

I landed my flyplane on the shoulder of an android picking up a Coke bottle on Amsterdam Avenue.

"Keep up the good work," I said over my loudspeaker.

He didn't hear me. He was listening on his iPod to Nikki playing her violin solo back in her bedroom. He was captivated by *The Music of the Spheres.*

Using his right hip, he nudged a garbage can set on rollers across the street. Passersby didn't realize that the garbage can was connected to his body. Whenever he tossed a bottle or can or newspaper into it, the recyclables got sucked through a hose and deposited directly into the android. There was a flap on his right hip, which allowed him to remove the hose and seem perfectly normal while strolling alongside other pedestrians.

Toshi and I planted the mini-lemonade carts around the island and unshrank them. Androids programmed to be vendors wheeled their carts off, chanting, "Lemonade for sale. Lemonade for sale."

The androids that were cleaning took a lemonade break every hour.

Once we reached our goal of one thousand androids, they would stop reproducing. Instead, all the recyclables they collected would be used to produce trees. Glass and plastic are made out of petroleum. Petroleum is energy. The lemonade and *The Music of the Spheres* were also forms of energy. All that energy combined would help fuel the transformation of discarded paper back into shimmering leaves and long, flowing branches.

Each android had to collect one thousand pounds of recyclables in order to produce a tree. Bobby kept track of their numbers back at command and control. Lucky he was doing that because my mind was on the girl with lovely little sky fingers.

As soon we save the planet, I'm asking Tula out on a date, DubDub.

That sounds like a good strategy, Giles.

Bobby's voice crackled in my ear while I soared over Times Square. "We've got a problem, Giles."

"What's up?" I said.

"Big Daddy's in big trouble. He's in a Mob bar down in Little Italy."

"What's Big Daddy doing in a Mob bar?" I asked.

"I don't know. But go check it out."

I found the android in a seedy pool hall, standing toe to toe with a three-hundred-pound mobster who was also named Big Daddy.

"Who's this, Big Daddy?" asked a gangster who had a scar running down his face.

"Some idiot," muttered the giant mobster.

The android glared up at the giant. "How dare you call yourself Big Daddy?"

"Dude, I'd shut up if I were you," the giant grunted, chalking a pool cue.

I sat in my flyplane on top of the eight ball, undetected.

"I am the one and only Big Daddy," proclaimed the android in a squeaky voice.

All the mobsters burst out laughing.

"You're Big Daddy?" said Scar Man. "Buddy, you're four feet tall."

The android didn't back down. "If there's one thing I can't stand, it's a fake Big Daddy."

The room fell silent.

"He just called Big Daddy a fake," said Scar Man. "Prepare to die."

The giant snarled. The other gangsters circled the android, whipping out switchblades and brass knuckles.

The giant swung his pool cue. In an instant I shrunk the Eco-droid down. The giant's pool cue whacked Scar Man on the side the head. Blood dripping onto his leather vest, Scar Man grabbed a platter of chicken wings off the bar and shoved them in the giant's face. A brawl erupted. I stuffed the android into the copilot's seat of my flyplane and darted out the window, colliding with a buffalo wing along the way.

"Oh, great," I said. "Now I've got buffalo wing sauce all over my flyplane. Thank's a lot, Big Daddy."

"I'm calling the police," the droid muttered. "How many years do you get if you're a fake Big Daddy? It better be at least fifty. Without parole."

"I'm supposed to be a superhero. Superheroes don't smell like chicken wings."

"You'll be the first," he said. "There's nothing wrong with being original."

"There's nothing wrong with obeying the rules either," I said. "You're supposed to be cleaning the streets of Manhattan."

"Big Daddy doesn't clean," insisted the android. "Big Daddy is a progenitor."

"A progeni-what?"

"Progenitor. He gives birth to droids. Have you ever heard of a queen bee, Giles?"

"Of course I've heard of a queen bee, you stupid droid."

"The queen bee doesn't do anything. She just sits around all day while the other bees work their butts off. Big Daddy's the same way." The android glowed haughtily. "I'm like a queen bee. But I'm Big Daddy."

"I'm telling Tula."

"Go right ahead."

I got ahold of Tula. Her cotton candy hair hardly fit on my monitor.

"Big Daddy said he doesn't clean, Tula."

"That's correct, Giles. Big Daddy will not turn into a

tree like the other androids. Instead, he will move on to other cities around your planet and give birth to new armies of Eco-droids."

"Wait. Hold on a second. Did you say the Eco-droids are going to turn into trees?"

"You didn't know that?" she said.

"Well . . . no. I mean I knew they had environmental-reversal software that could turn paper back into trees. But I had no idea *they'd* actually turn into trees. I mean the droids themselves. That's like the coolest thing I've ever heard."

"They will become a permanent part of the city, Giles. An enduring reminder of all your species can do when it tries."

"Will they have to be watered with lemonade? They need it now, don't they?"

"Yes, but once they turn into trees they will only require water, just like normal trees."

"Call me an idiot, but I still don't understand how they'll turn into trees."

"The heart of every android is a greenhouse," Tula said. "Show Giles, Big Daddy."

Big Daddy opened himself up. His torso parted like the doors of a china cabinet. Down where human intestines would be, a platinum engine threw off waves of shimmering light. It was connected to a tube running up to his throat. This is where the lemonade went. Any glass and plastic that got sucked into his body also ended up here in the Energy Center, my lawyer explained.

"Do you see the seed, Giles?" Tula said. "All the paper gets shrunken down and stored inside it."

Big Daddy's heart, a glass greenhouse, contained a seed in the center, sitting on a golden pedestal.

"That tiny seed can store up to one thousand pounds

of paper," Tula said. "Tonight, at the stroke of midnight, all the seeds in all the droids will pop like popcorn kernels. Thanks to the Energy Center. Presto, you'll have five million leaves."

"But my seed won't pop," said the pain-in-the-butt android.

"I wish you'd turn into a tree right now," I said. "Then you'd stop bothering me."

"Don't forget, Giles," Tula said. "Everything started with Big Daddy. You wouldn't have an army of Eco-droids if it wasn't for him."

"That's right," said the android.

"OK, OK," I said. "Now what am I supposed to do with him, Tula? I have to get back to work."

"Let him wander around the city. Big Daddy, if you don't behave I'll tell Dr. Sprinkles. She'll reduce your personality."

"I don't want to be boring!" cried the android.

"Then be a good droid," Tula said.

"When are you coming back to Earth, Tula?" I asked.

"I'm not sure. I'm at the hospital right now. We've got a major crisis going on."

"What happened?" I asked.

"I'm representing a planet called Nawdry in the Salvakian Galaxy. A neighboring planet has been dumping refuse on Nawdry's moon. We're finally about to go to trial but one of the jurors just got rushed to ER. One of his heads had a brain aneurysm."

"How many heads does he have?" I asked.

"Three."

"A three-headed juror?" I said.

"We have to decide if he's still fit to be a juror with only two heads. There's always something to deal with. Bye, Giles. Good luck."

"I miss you," I said.

"I miss you too."

Her face dissolved on the monitor.

Big Daddy's squeaky voice took on a teasing tone. "Giles misses his girlfriend. How cute."

"All right. I've had enough of you."

I dropped him off in Chinatown and rejoined Toshi down by South Street Seaport. We spent the next half hour removing graffiti. Making skyscrapers immaculate burns fuel fast.

My gas gauge flickered on EMPTY. I did a nosedive, landing in a pothole. DubDub gave me a riddle.

If Bobby ate a bad burrito, what would you say in church?

I'd say a prayer for Bobby's underwear.

Correct, Giles.

The needle shot back up to FULL.

I got my butt, which was about the size of a pencil eraser, back up there eliminating graffiti, making the metropolis immaculate. At dawn, a flood of golden light made Manhattan look even more pristine.

My big brother's voice echoed inside my glistening spacecraft. "Giles, Stanley wants to know if you need a copilot."

"No!" I said. "I just got rid of Big Daddy."

"Please come get him," Bobby begged. "He's driving me crazy."

"He's your assistant, Bobby."

"I don't need an assistant."

"Why did Dr. Sprinkles ever give me something so lame?" I said. "He's completely useless."

"I heard that," Stanley said.

I forgot he had an intercom.

"I was just kidding, Stanley," I said.

"Sure you were."

There was silence while the parking meter pouted.

"Hey, I've got a job for you," I said. "You can do surveillance. You've got wheels. Roll around the city and keep an eye on things."

"That's a great idea," Bobby said. "We'll give you some cloudfish cover. A moving parking meter might freak people out."

"How does that sound, Stanley?" I said.

"OK," the meter mumbled, still reeling from the insult.

Apart from hurting Stanley's feelings, everything was going remarkably well. Toshi and I now patrolled the subways for graffiti. We removed all of it from aboveground by eight in the morning.

We didn't take the cloudfish down below because people might've mistaken them for smoke and thought there was a fire. We didn't want to incite a panic. Fortunately the subways were rarely crowded on a Sunday. We didn't have to deal with rush hour. Also, many New Yorkers fled the city in July to escape the heat. Those who couldn't afford to go on vacation were dazed by the mugginess.

When three sweaty people stumbled onto the Number 6 train, I gave a public service announcement over the loudspeaker on my flyplane: "WARNING. DUE TO HEAT EXHAUSTION YOU MAY START TO HALLUCINATE. IF YOU SEE SOMETHING STRANGE, PAY NO ATTENTION TO IT. JUST GO HOME AND DRINK SOME ICE WATER."

The odd thing was, no one paid any attention to the graffiti removal taking place on the ceiling. They were all staring down at their smart phones. Thank God for texting.

With my phenomenally efficient flyplane, I cleaned an entire subway station in no time flat. I was ahead of schedule and having the time of my life when Navida called.

"Giles, what do you make of these street cleaners? Everyone's talking about them."

"Just don't get in their way," I warned her. "Whatever you do, don't get in their way."

"And what about this weird fog? It's otherworldly."

"It seems pretty worldly to me," I said.

"Something big is going on. Isn't it, Giles?"

"I'm not allowed to say."

"Did they ask you not to divulge their identity?"

"No comment."

"Could the future of the planet be put in jeopardy if you told me?"

"Maybe."

"All right, Giles. I won't ask any more questions."

"I think that's a good idea, Navida."

"I'll post it on my blog. Don't mess with the street cleaners."

"Now you're talking," I said.

"I have to go, Giles. We're turning a vacant lot into a community garden."

Apparently some rich girl begged her daddy to donate the land. He was a real estate tycoon. She got inspired to do something environmentally responsible after getting drenched by the commercial for Navida's blog. The guy gave his daughter a vacant lot and an ice cream cake for her birthday.

The land was worth millions of dollars. I discussed all this with my flyplane as we soared up out of the subway station at eleven in the morning, heading over to the vacant lot.

See, DubDub. There are good people in this world. Not everyone is a selfish, greedy, pathetic fool.

What a pleasant surprise, Giles.

The lot was over on Avenue B. It didn't feel like I was wasting time. Navida was an unofficial member of our team. I was keeping an eye on a team member. That was my part of my job, right?

A couple of hundred kids were gathered at the vacant lot. I found Navida in the crowd, a pretty Puerto Rican girl in a wheelchair, her pyramid-shaped earrings swaying in the breeze, her sphinx necklace glimmering.

Navida had a rare disease. The doctors said it wasn't going to kill her but it made her life pretty hard. She used to go to my school but had to drop out to do homeschooling.

I perched on her shoulder in my flyplane. Mosquitoes swarmed around her. Mosquitoes who pick on people in wheelchairs are the lowest of the low. It took a lot of self-restraint not to annihilate them. DubDub sprayed them with a special repellant that made them only bite people who litter. They took off in search of bozos tossing hot dog wrappers on the sidewalk.

Using my amplifier without her knowing, I helped Navida's frail voice boom across the vacant lot. "OK, everyone. Let's turn this junk heap into a little piece of paradise."

While a bunch of kids scooped up broken glass with shovels, a nerdy guy tried to lift a rusty old refrigerator by himself.

A jock in a Mets jersey laughed at him. "Dude, like you could really lift that all by yourself."

I flew into the nerd's ear and said over the loudspeaker, "Dude, try to lift it again."

It freaked him out. "Who said that?"

"Just do it."

Kneeling down, he tried with all his might to lift the fridge. The fridge rose up into the air, with DubDub's help of course. It looked as though the nerd was balancing a refrigerator on the tip of one finger. He tossed it effortlessly into a Dumpster.

The jock was stunned. "Dude, how did you do that?"

Half a dozen cute girls surrounded the nerd.

"How did you get to be so strong?" one asked.

"Chocolate milk," he said. "I drink half a gallon a day."

"Do you put protein powder in it?" asked the jock.

"No. I drink it straight."

On the other side of the vacant lot, Navida was barking out orders. "Hey, you guys, there's still some broken glass over here. Come on. Let's get moving."

When they finally got everything cleaned up and planted some seeds in the soil, someone handed the birthday girl a rainbow-colored watering can to sprinkle on the seeds.

She handed it to Navida. "No," she said, "you do it, Navida. If it wasn't for you and your blog none of us would be here right now."

Everyone cheered for Navida.

Hanging upside down in my flyplane from her earring, I overheard her whisper to herself, "I'm going to imagine that this water came from the Nile."

In ten seconds flat I shot over to Egypt, swooped down in

between two Bedouins and a camel and landed on a hippo's back in the middle of the Nile River.

"What's up, hippo?" I said while DubDub collected a drop of water.

We raced back to the Big Apple and squeezed the drop into the watering can just as Navida sprinkled it all over the soil.

When you're a superhero, you can do stuff like that.

Superheroes also deal with trouble. We had some brewing. Toshi spotted it first. He said the androids were starting to create a spectacle. A crowd had gathered on the corner of Fifth Avenue and Fifty-fifth Street, eyes fixed on a tall figure in blue overalls. He spotted a candy wrapper floating down from the top of Trump Tower. Rather than waiting for it to reach his outstretched hands, he took a running leap onto a park bench and vaulted himself into the air, grabbing the red wrapper high above a green traffic light. He did a back flip on his way down and landed on top of a cab. The crowd cheered madly while the cabbie swore in Russian.

"Look," said an Italian tourist, "I caught it on my iPhone." He showed his wife the video.

"Great," I told Toshi. "Now we're going to be all over YouTube."

"We already are," Toshi said. "One clip already had thirty thousand hits. People all over the world are checking this out."

As if that wasn't enough, two hundred tourists aimed their camcorders at another android who climbed up the side of a brownstone like Spider-Man to snatch a paper bag out of some ivy.

He was listening to *The Music of the Spheres* on his iPod. Swooping in my flyplane, I dislodged his earphones, flew into his ear and said over the loudspeaker, "Dude, you obviously love your job. I appreciate that. But you're way too acrobatic. This isn't Cirque du Soleil."

He ignored me.

I landed DubDub behind a newspaper stand and returned to my normal size under cloudfish camouflage.

I rushed over to the street cleaner. "Dude, it's me, Giles. I'm in charge here. You need to calm down. Humans can't fly, OK?"

"I'm sorry," said the android. "I can't hear you. I'm listening to music."

He marched away.

A little boy ran over to him, waving a pen and paper. "Can I have your autograph?"

Toshi shook his head. "That's the first time I've ever seen anyone ask a garbage man for an autograph."

"I'm sorry," the android told the kid. "I have to go drink lemonade."

He nudged his garbage can across the busy intersection.

"What are we going to do about this?" I said.

"I don't know," said Toshi. "There aren't enough cloudfish to conceal all the street cleaners."

While we stood there pondering our dilemma, someone said, "I think they're robots."

Toshi and I turned around.

It was an old man.

Toshi snickered. "That's a good one."

"Yeah," I said, emitting a fake laugh, "there's an army of robots cleaning New York City."

"Did you see it climb up the side of that building?" the man asked.

"It had suction cups, sir," Toshi said.

"Yeah," I said. "What's the big deal?"

"Why do they breathe so strangely?" the old man said.

"Sounds perfectly normal to me," I said.

"Me too," agreed Toshi.

"I'm telling you," he muttered. "They're robots."

"Robots don't go around picking up trash off the streets of New York," Toshi said.

"Look at Wall-E. He was a robot. He went around picking up trash."

That was an insult I just couldn't tolerate. "Listen, buddy," I said. "I loved that movie too. But these are intergalactic Eco-droids. They can turn paper back into trees. They're far more powerful than a man-made robot like Wall-E."

I couldn't believe I said it.

Toshi pulled me aside and hissed, "Dude, what is wrong with you?"

I gave another fake laugh to the old man. "Just kidding."

He didn't believe me.

Toshi jumped in. "I don't mean to be disrespectful, sir. But you're a grown man talking about robots. Aren't you supposed to be setting an example for us kids."

"That's right," I said. "We look to you for guidance, sir."

He looked us up and down. "Who are you?"

Toshi did the talking. It was safer. "I'm a dancer. He's a poet. We're geeks, OK? We live in a complete and total fantasy world."

"Seriously," he said. "Who are you?"

"Nevermind," Toshi said, yanking me down the street. "We have to go."

The old man followed us. "What planet are you from?"

"Earth," Toshi said. "Just like you."

"Where are the cleaners from?" he asked.

Toshi stopped, a sly look on his face. "Listen, if you want to know the truth, we don't even exist."

"You're hallucinating," I said.

"It's the heatwave," Toshi said.

"It's messing with your brain," I told him.

"You're talking to yourself right now," Toshi said.

"It's embarrassing," I said.

We managed to lose him in a wave of tourists. We shrank down and took off in the flyplanes in search of four-letter words spray-painted on deli signs.

Man, did I ever screw up.

Even the cloudfish got on my case, skywriting: THAT WAS PRETTY STUPID, GILES!

What would Tula think? Now I'd never get a kiss. No way. She'd never kiss a mouth this big.

"Do you think he'll tell other adults?" I asked Toshi over the intercom.

"Probably," he said. "But who's to say they'll believe him."

Before we could stress out about it, Bobby gave us an even bigger problem to deal with. "The lemonade vendors are getting arrested down in Washington Square Park."

We shot down to Greenwich Village.

CHAPTER TWENTY

WE UNSHRANK OURSELVES and rushed over to defend a street cleaner who was getting hassled by a burly bearded cop.

"Do you have a permit to sell lemonade?" asked the cop.

"A permit?" asked the vendor, circling his cart in a jittery, mechanical, un-human way. "What's . . . what's that?"

I hoped that cop didn't have good eyesight.

"Come with me," he said. "You're under arrest."

"Leave him alone," I said.

The cop eyed me sternly. "Son, mind your own business."

"There's a heat wave, officer," I blurted. "People will die of thirst without lemonade."

He rested his hand on his holster. "Son, don't make me shoot you." He shifted his attention back to the vendor.

"Wait, hold on a second," Toshi whispered. "What kind of cop would threaten to shoot a thirteen-year-old kid?"

"Those aren't real cops, Toshi. They're droid cops. Look at their faces. Look at that weird twitch. They all have it."

"Droids arresting droids," he said.

"I bet they work for Petulance," I said.

"She planted a black butterfly," he said. "I guess she could plant droids."

The cop handcuffed the vendor and stuffed him into the back of a squad car. Another cop wheeled the lemonade cart up a ramp onto the back of a flatbed truck already loaded with fifteen other carts.

We ducked behind a statue, did a quick shrink, hopped in the flyplanes and took off after a convoy of twenty squad cars and three flatbed trucks. Speeding through a red light, they disappeared. How does a convoy of squad cars disappear in the blink of an eye?

"They must've gone through an envelope in space," Toshi said over my intercom.

"Into a parallel universe," I said.

DubDub interrupted us.

My sensors have confirmed Toshi's theory, Giles. They went through an envelope in space. However, I do believe that the vendors are still on the island of Manhattan.

Great, DubDub. Where?

I'm afraid I don't know, Giles.

"Hey, Giles," Toshi said, "how long can the street cleaners survive without lemonade?"

"One hour."

It was 1:26 p.m.

According to DubDub, it had been twenty-six minutes since their last break. That gave us thirty-four minutes to find them.

I contacted Bobby in command and control. "Bobby, we lost them."

"So did I," Bobby said.

We searched in vain up and down Manhattan. Now we

only had a quarter of an hour. In fifteen minutes, one by one, the androids would drop dead on the city streets. In fifteen minutes we'd fail the test. Fifteen minutes until the end of the world. Fifteen minutes until the hairy cages.

"I found them!" Bobby's triumphant voice made my helmet rattle. "Or should I say Stanley found them."

"Stanley?" I said in utter astonishment. "No way."

"That was a good idea to have him do surveillance, Giles. He's on the corner of Tenth Avenue and Fourteenth Street. Go pick him up."

I sped over there, shrank Stanley down under cloudfish cover and heaved him into my copilot's seat. Now that he had actually done something heroic, did he ever have an attitude. He was the most pompous parking meter of all time.

"What good is a parking meter?" he said in a mocking tone. "Useless. That's what I am. Useless."

I kept my mouth shut.

He went on. "A parking meter can't do anything. Like a parking meter is really going to help me save the world. This is the lamest gadget I've ever seen in my life." He was impersonating me, Giles. I have to say. He was pretty good.

"OK, OK," I said. "I'm sorry I said you were useless."

"Apologize for calling me lame."

"I'm sorry I called you lame."

"Say, 'I wish I was a parking meter.'"

"I'm not saying that."

"Say it or I'm not showing you where the vendors are."

"OK. OK. I wish I was a parking meter."

"Say, 'I wish I could spit quarters at bad guys.'"

"I wish I could spit quarters at bad guys. There. Are you satisfied?"

"Make a left at the next corner."

The vendors were being held hostage in a recycling center over by the West Side Highway.

One of the fake cops was operating a crane with a giant scooper attached to its end. Dozens of Eco-droids and lemonade carts were crammed inside the scooper, which hovered perilously in the air above a machine used to shred recycled materials. As soon they got dropped into the shredder, our droids would be crunched, squashed and pulverized. They'd come out the other end as balls of paper, glass and plastic.

Cable, the princess's goon with the plasma TV skin, was in charge of this operation. He sat in a leather recliner off to the side, surrounded by droid cops, leering at our helpless vendors.

Even on the brink of death, one of the vendors still chanted, "Lemonade for sale. Lemonade for sale."

"Will you please hurry up and crush those things," Cable told the cop in the crane. "They're really getting on my nerves."

Toshi and I perched on a windowsill in our flyplanes.

"We need to move fast, Toshi. You take out the droid cop driving the crane. I'll go after Cable."

"Got it."

"What's my job?" whispered Stanley, sitting alongside me.

"Um . . . Stanley, you spit quarters at the other cops."

"I will be unmerciful," said the parking meter.

"You do that, Stanley," I said.

The thrill of battle made my miniature body hum and tingle. By rescuing the vendors, I could make up for blabbing to the old man.

"OK, guys," I said. "On three. One . . . two . . ."

Just as we were about to launch our attack, Tula showed up with two dozen armored SWAT creatures, each one the size of a Cyclops. They immediately disarmed the droid cops and yanked the crane operator out of his little cabin.

Tula marched over to the groupie. "Cable," Tula said, "these are marshals from the Halls of Universal Justice. You're under arrest. Anything you say can and will be used against you."

"I'm not saying a word," Cable grunted.

A black-and-white image of Jimmy Cagney flashed across Cable's television body. Cagney was a famous bad guy movie star from long ago. My dad has a bunch of his DVDs. Now he appeared on Cable's forehead, snarling at Tula. "You can't arrest me, copper."

I had to admit. It was pretty clever. Cable kept his mouth shut while a character from an old gangster movie spoke on his behalf. These weren't words from a movie. Cable was somehow putting lines in Cagney's mouth.

Jimmy Cagney shrugged at the lemonade vendors, who were being helped out of the scooper along with their carts. "I know the law, copper. These Eco-droids are made from re-cycled materials. I'm allowed to keep them at a recycling cen-ter." He snickered in black-and-white. "I'm doing my civic duty, copper. I'm an environmentally responsible gangster."

"We're not arresting you for droid abduction," Tula said.

"Then why are you arresting me?"

"You forgot to pay your cable bill."

"You're arresting me for that, copper?"

"It's six months overdue. That's an intergalactic misde-meanor." Tula grinned. "By the time the princess bails you out, the humans will already have passed the test."

Three lobster cloudfish poured through an air vent and etched a message above the groupie: YOU'RE GOING TO JAIL, DUDE!

Cable ignored it. His eyes were fixed on me. Now he did the talking, not Jimmy Cagney. "You couldn't take me down on your own. Could you, Giles? You needed the help of a girl."

"Get this loser out of here," Tula told the marshals.

"Look, Giles," Cable said, pointing at his arm.

There I was, on his TV skin, standing in the elevator with Toshi and Buck.

"In this week's episoded of *Giles, The Coward*," Cable said, "Giles won't even attempt to defend himself from the super's son."

"Don't look, Giles," warned Tula. "That arm has the power to reveal your darkest fears."

The cloudfish tried to block the screen from view but for some reason I could see through the mist. I saw Buck grab me by the throat. I handed over sixty dollars without a fight. I was watching a television show of my own cowardice.

"That's why your lawyer came to save the day, Giles," Cable said. "She thinks you're a wimp, dude. Your own girlfriend thinks you're a wimp."

The police droids chuckled.

I had a sick feeling that the Bridgelings were watching. They could see all the way across the universe. That's how good their vision was. Tears slid down one hundred eyes as they watched me act like a wimp.

Pulling me away from Cable, Tula led me into a back office and squeezed my hand. "I don't think you're a wimp, Giles."

"Then why didn't you let me rescue the vendors?" I asked.

"I thought you wanted my help."

"Who says I need your help?"

"You yelled at me in the elevator for not helping you with Buck."

"That was different. Now I've got a flyplane. I've got Toshi. I'm a . . ."

"You're a what, Giles?"

I knew she'd nail me if I said superhero.

"Nevermind," I said. "Let's just get one thing straight. I don't need you stepping in and saving the day."

"You can handle any situation on your own?"

"You're darn right I can."

"Giles, you have a serious attitude problem."

I gagged. "You sound like my math teacher."

"Giles, you sound like someone who is spiraling out of control. You have one chance to save this planet." She jabbed a blue finger into my chest. "Don't screw it up."

CHAPTER TWENTY-ONE

ERASING GRAFFITI in the grimy gloom of a subway tunnel, my flyplane wouldn't shut up.

Giles, your lawyer possesses a wisdom beyond her years.

Are you saying she's right and I'm wrong, DubDub?

No, Giles.

That's good. 'Cuz you're my flyplane. I hope we don't have any loyalty issues.

Giles, it would be an act of betrayal if I failed to point out that you may be getting a little carried away by thinking of yourself as a super . . .

I hate the way you can read my mind. Just shut up and get rid of the graffiti.

As you say, Giles.

I fantasized about having dinner at the White House after the president found out I saved the human race. As a show of gratitude, he gave me fifty millions dollars, a private jet and a lifetime supply of s'mores. I shook his hand, told him what a swell guy he was and flew off to the Halls of Universal Justice to walk across the Bridgeling.

I couldn't wait for that to happen in real life. Where would the Bridgeling take me once I crossed it? What new worlds would I explore?

If I recited a poem while walking across it, what would happen? Would I end up in a galaxy where everyone rhymes? I wouldn't mind going there.

Although DubDub annoyed me with his lecturing, he did do an awesome job cleaning subways. I loved my fly-plane. By six p.m.—with Toshi's help, of course—the entire subway system was almost immaculate.

The word *Death* was the last bit of graffiti on the island of Manhattan. The bloodred letters ran down a pillar on a subway platform at Union Square.

I erased it.

The graffiti was gone, but not the muggers. They were still around, like the guy on the Number 4 train up ahead. He snuck up on a yawning woman in a nurse's outfit. She looked so tired, not even the roar of the train could keep her from dozing off. She was the only one in the subway car, except for the pickpocket. When she fell fast asleep, he silently grabbed her purse. Big mistake. Don't try to pull that on my patrol.

He crept through the connecting doors into an empty car. I followed him, darted up ahead, spun around and flew right at his chest, ramming him at full speed. He gasped and wheezed and crumpled to the floor. He slowly got up and looked around wildly to see who hit him. I nailed him again, a crushing blow that hurled him halfway across the car. DubDub sure packed a big wallop for being miniature. When the thief fell, he spilled the nurse's purse all over the floor.

I picked up a five-dollar bill with a pair of ultra-strong robot pincers disguised as the spindly legs of a housefly. I activated DubDub's loudspeaker and yelled into it, my voice distorted by some really cool special effects. The pickpocket thought the five-dollar bill was talking to him. You should've seen the look on his face.

"I BELONG TO HER! I BELONG TO HER!" I howled in the creepiest voice you ever heard, a cross between Darth Vader and Freddy Krueger. "DO YOU HEAR ME, PUNK?"

"Yeah, I hear you," he whimpered.

"DUDE, WHAT'S WRONG WITH YOU? YOU'RE TALKING TO A FIVE-DOLLAR BILL."

He couldn't take his eyes off the floating fiver. It freaked him out.

"GO GIVE THE LADY BACK HER PURSE. AND GIVE HER ALL YOUR MONEY TOO."

"I'm not givin' her my money. Man, are you crazy?"

I slammed him against the wall.

"DUDE, YOU JUST GOT YOUR BUTT KICKED BY A HOUSEFLY. THAT'S EMBARRASSING."

He pulled out his wallet, dumped all his cash into her purse, tiptoed back into the adjacent car and placed the purse in her lap. She kept sleeping the whole time.

I flew into the mugger's ear and whispered, "All right. Now get outta here, punk. And don't let me catch you stealing again."

When the sliding doors opened at the next stop, he ran for his life.

I shot down the subway tunnel, just to check it out. Superheroes have to go exploring every now and then. Right?

Using night vision, I found an abandoned station full of bats, thousands of them, hanging upside down, fast asleep.

I bet bats sleep right side up on the Upside Downers planet. Don't they, DubDub?

That's correct, Giles.

We floated through the vast cave, careful not to make a sound. After all, bats eat flies.

Hey DubDub, this is like a cheeseburger sneaking through a house full of fat people.

Giles, I don't think there's another imagination like yours in the entire universe.

Bats in clusters clung to the moldy ceiling. They draped from rusty pipes.

Let's wake them up, DubDub.

Please no, Giles. You're on a quest.

I know. But we got rid of all the graffiti, didn't we?

That's just the beginning, Giles. The trees have not been created yet.

We'll only let them chase us for a minute or two.

I flicked on the loudspeaker, impersonating a guy at a drive-thru. "Hello. Can I take your order?"

Bats stirred. Ears twitched. Wings unfurled. Soft squeaks pierced the silence. I saw a pair of beady bat eyes bulging from a crumpled bat face.

"Hey, dude," I said, "I'd hide in a cave too if I was that ugly."

The chase was on. One hundred bats swarmed down the tunnel behind me, billowing like a black tornado.

Of course, none of them could catch me. All except for one.

That bat sure is fast, DubDub.

That's not a real bat, Giles. It's a star cruiser disguised as a bat.

I was afraid you might say that.

DubDub activated a surveillance camera on his thorax, and an image flashed across my monitor. It was Heads-or-Tails, the worshipper of Princess Petulance, closing in out of the blackness, firing a laser from his curlicue tail.

"A bat-shaped spaceship driven by a pig with no body," I moaned. "Only in New York."

We dodged the laser and the falling debris that came showering down when the boar blasted the ceiling.

"Bobby, I'm under attack," I screamed over the intercom.

My brother didn't respond. Was he paying me back for the book title?

"I'll change the title, Bobby. I swear. Just talk to me."

Nothing.

"Toshi, can you hear me?"

Again nothing. My communication system had been sabotaged. DubDub and I were all alone deep beneath the earth.

Ducking through a crack in the floor, we descended for what felt like miles into a maze-like sewer system, a dark, dripping labyrinth of drains and pipes.

Were my brother and sister wondering where I was? Or did they expect this from me? They'd seen me wander off, get distracted and mess up countless times before. If I was a failure then, why wouldn't I be one now?

The flying pig was nowhere in sight. But of all people

to bump into, Jerry, the sleazy alien realtor, was taking a leisurely stroll through the sewer. He knew exactly where I was, despite my tiny size. "Hey, Giles, aren't you supposed to be cleaning Manhattan?"

"Hey, Jerry," I said over my loudspeaker, "you're in a sewer. Right where you belong."

"Precious time is ticking away, Giles."

He didn't need to remind me. I was well aware. It was already seven o'clock. Only five hours left.

"Why don't you just give up, Giles? Face the inevitable. You're outta here!"

"I'm never giving up, Jerry."

My communication system was down but Jerry's wasn't. He got a phone call.

"It's not my fault there's acid rain falling on your new condo," he said to the alien on the other end of the line. "I don't make the weather on Pluto, sir." He turned irate. "Don't report me to the Better Business Bureau. I'll be right there." He hung up and fixed his beady eyes on me. "I have to go, Giles. I wanted to watch you die. Oh well. You can't have everything."

As soon as he left, Heads-or-Tails came in for the kill, firing his laser at some drain pipes overhead. They crashed down on DubDub. We righted ourselves and spun around, wobbling, speeding off through the gloom.

All this because I had to go off searching for bats. I was like a big chocolate eyeball on the face of Dr. Sprinkles. While Bobby and the rest of my team went in one direction, like the doctor's nose and mouth and other eye, I took off somewhere else.

That's me. Giles, the big chocolate eyeball.

(Hey, reader, can a big chocolate eyeball be a superhero? Wait, don't answer that.)

There was a bend up ahead. Rounding the corner, Dub-Dub came to a jarring halt. I smashed my head against the console.

I lifted my head groggily, peered out the window and rubbed my eyes in disbelief. My flyplane was caught in a humongous spider web. It was made out of barbed wire. What kind of spider spun a barbed-wire web? Not the kind of spider I had any desire to come in contact with.

The pig hung merrily from the ceiling in his bat-cruiser while DubDub tried in vain to free himself from the web.

"Hey, Giles," the boar squealed over his own loudspeaker, "look on the bright side. At least you won't get sent to De-soleen."

"Only an idiot would have his body removed to lose weight," I yelled back. "Why didn't you join a health club, you bozo?"

Have you ever been punched by a smell? Well, I have. Just then I got punched in the nose by a stench. I gagged. Was I smelling my own death? Was I smelling my failure to pull off this quest? Was I smelling the end of the world? Why did I have tragic thoughts like that? Why couldn't I have a normal brain? Why did I have to have the weird brain of a poet? Poets think about death all the time. Look at Shakespeare. That's all the dude ever talks about. If you take death out of Shakespeare, all you've got is a couple of where-for-art-thous.

I glanced down at a puddle that rippled like a little swamp. Two bright yellow eyes drifted on the surface of the puddle, staring up at me. Slowly the monster rose up out of the water. The word *bizarre* seemed insufficient. This creature had the head and tail of an alligator and the body of a colossal spider.

What is it, DubDub?

A munyateeka.

I'd call it a gatorantula, DubDub. I heard there were alligators living in the sewers but this is going overboard.

Munyateekas aren't native to your planet, Giles. They come from the Bek Star System.

A hologram of Princess Petulance flickered above the web. "How do you like my munyateeka, Giles?" she said.

"It's better looking than you are," I yelled back.

"Just think," she said, "you could've been a prince. You could've had your own kingdom. Every kangaroo on this planet would've belonged to you. Every koala bear would've been your loyal subject. The Great Barrier Reef would've been your swimming pool. But you had to go and blow it."

The munyateeka climbed onto the web, crawling in my direction. DubDub cut a hole in the web with his laser. The monster patched the hole before we could escape, shooting strands of barbed wire out of its long green tail.

Although unable to free himself entirely, DubDub was able to squirm around the web, avoiding the gaping jaws of the alien predator.

Unfortunately we came to a dead stop in the center of the web.

What's wrong, DubDub?

I'm out of fuel.

Not now, DubDub.

I'm sorry, Giles.

OK. What's the riddle?

Who got sticky at the picnic?

Why can't you be solar powered like Superfly?

Who got sticky at the picnic, Giles?

I don't care about a stupid picnic. I'm about to get chomped on by a gatorantula. Let me tell you something, DubDub. When you're about to get chomped on by a gatorantula it's really hard to rhyme.

The monster inched closer.

Giles, who got sticky at the picnic?

My rhymer isn't working, DubDub. I've got a broken rhymer.

Who got sticky at the picnic?

I did.

Incorrect, Giles.

Grandma. She was putting relish on the hot dogs and her hands got sticky.

Incorrect. Who got sticky at the picnic?

The munyateeka was upon us.

I got! I got it, DubDub! Nikki got sticky at the picnic!

We had a full tank of gas.

DubDub blasted the monster with his laser. The creature doubled in size, as if the laser was gatorantula food.

That wasn't the outcome I was hoping for, Giles.

Me either, DubDub.

I'm going to eject you, Giles.

But what about you?

Don't worry about me.

I am worried about you, DubDub.

Good-bye, Giles.

You're the best star cruiser ever.

Thank you, Giles.

I got catapulted out of the cockpit just as the monster took a big bite.

"Great," I cried, "my flyplane got eaten by a gatorantula."

It was such a bummer. But I didn't have time to worry about it because the rats were coming.

CHAPTER TWENTY-TWO

THEY POURED OUT of holes in the wall. They wriggled out of cracks in the floor. They were authentic New York City sewer rats. That didn't make me feel any better. These rodents made robot rats look like gerbils.

I took off running. Should I unshrink myself? The rats wouldn't mess with me then. But if I was big the gatorantula could spot me easily. It was right behind the rats, scuttling through the sewer. I didn't know what to do.

Big hungry sewer rats can make you feel confused. I splashed through the muck. I dashed down a slimy tunnel.

I came to a place where three tunnels met. I paused for a moment, trying to decide which way to go. A rat pounced. It had me by the wrist. My life was over. Dead at thirteen. Man, did that ever suck. What sucked even more was that I would never get a chance to apologize to Tula.

I'd never get that kiss.

I had to get that kiss.

I fought and screamed and wriggled and writhed while it gnawed off my hand. Why wasn't this hurting? How can you lose a hand and not be in agony? As I stared down at its frothing fangs, I realized that they hadn't punctured my skin. Instead, they were biting off the S/U. The gadget was made out of some alien plastic which the rat had a hard time severing. If it hadn't been for the S/U, I would've been dead. The rat kept working on it. When it finally fell off my wrist, I threw it at the rat and took off running.

The only problem with losing my S/U was that I was stuck being miniature.

I ducked into a rat hole. They were all out looking for me, leaving their den empty. I followed a passage littered with bones and feathers. Everywhere you looked there were bones and feathers.

Those poor pigeons.

I fled deeper into the hole, finally emerging into a long passageway.

A rat crawled out from underneath a rusty bucket. I darted in the other direction, panting, sweating, trying to catch my breath, trying to keep running even though my feet were blistered.

I came to a towering oval door that looked as if it hadn't been opened for centuries. I was about to slide underneath it. I stopped. Rats were on the other side, coming for me, squeezing underneath, ready for dinner, for Giles-sushi, for a spicy Giles roll. Do you get miso soup with a spicy Giles roll? Why was I thinking about sushi at a time like this? I was going insane, that's why. Death will do that.

Suddenly a voice whispered from the top of the door. "Quick. Climb up."

A tiny rope ladder came spilling down. I climbed it frantically. It led to a keyhole in the door. It was an old-fashioned keyhole, the kind that a skeleton key would fit.

A teeny-weeny wiry hand pulled me into the keyhole and yanked up the rope ladder just as Heads-or-Tails flew down the passageway in the bat cruiser.

"You're safe now," said a gentle voice.

There was a miniature apartment inside the keyhole, a table and chairs and a couch set up in between the cogs and springs and levers in the door lock. It was cramped but cozy.

An alien smiled at me. Made out of tubes and wires, he was even smaller than me in my shrunken state.

"Who are you?" I asked, still panting.

"We're Keyholians," he said. "We migrated to Earth two thousand years ago after our planet became uninhabitable."

A gatorantula and Keyholians. Just another day in the life of me, Giles.

A lady alien stepped out from behind a bolt in the door lock. "Welcome, Giles."

"How do you know my name?"

"Everyone knows who you are," she said. "The fate of the planet rests on your shoulders."

A girl Keyholian glided into the room on a skateboard made from a half a toothpick.

"Who are you?" I asked.

"I'm Key-wee." She sniffed me and turned to her mother. "He stinks, Mommy. And he's ugly."

"Now that will be enough of that," snapped her father.

Key-wee sailed away on her skateboard. I wasn't sad to see her go.

Mrs. Keyholian took off my shoes and gently rubbed an ointment all over my aching feet. It smelled like peppermint and jasmine. My blisters disappeared.

"My flyplane got eaten by a gatorantula," I muttered. "I need to rescue it. I have to get out of here. You don't understand. We're running out of time. I only have until midnight. I'm going to wake up tomorrow on Desoleen. I don't have a second to waste. I've already wasted an hour and a half down here."

I came to the conclusion, right then and there, that my specialty in life was wasting time.

(Hey, reader, do you have too much time on your hands? Give it to me. I'll waste it for you. Just stuff it in a manila envelope and send it to The Big Chocolate Eyeball, New York, New York.)

"I'm afraid you'll need your lawyer's help to defeat the munyateeka, Giles," said Mr. Keyholian.

He knew I wasn't a superhero. I didn't blame him. I was just a kid with some gadgets. That's all. Real fancy gadgets. Extremely fancy gadgets. I kept telling myself that. Whenever the superhero thing popped into my head, I said it. I was just a kid with some gadgets. A kid who can't concentrate. A kid like that can't be a superhero. No way. I kept saying it. I didn't exactly believe it, but I kept saying it.

"Do you have a way of reaching Tula?" I asked Mr. Keyholian.

Opening a drawer, he pulled out what looked like a cross between an old typewriter, an accordion and an eight-track tape player. It had a rinky-dink set of antennae planted on top.

"Hold on a second," I said. "What's that thing? You guys are aliens. Aren't you supposed to be more high-tech?"

"We don't believe in technology," said Mrs. Keyholian. "It destroyed our planet. We had the most advanced civilization of all. But it didn't stop us from poisoning the soil, polluting the air and contaminating every keyhole."

"I'll send a message to the Keyholian who resides in your apartment," said Mr. Keyholian. "He will let Tula know where you are."

"We have Keyholians in our apartment?" I said.

"Yes, there's one in your front door. His name is Mitchell. He's a bachelor."

"Only a bachelor could fit in your keyhole," said Mrs. Keyholian.

"You have a new lock on your front door," her husband said, slamming an eight-track tape into the tape-player part of the contraption and pressing the play button. "It's extremely small."

"Modern locksmiths have no consideration for Keyholians whatsoever," added his wife.

The message sender began to hum loudly. Mr. Keyholian turned down the volume and tugged on his wiry beard. "We moved down here because this keyhole has more space. We didn't want to live down below. But we needed a larger apartment."

"Grandma lives with us," chirped Key-wee, plopping down on the couch.

She drew my attention to a little loft above the lock mechanism. Grandma Keyholian was sitting up in bed, knitting a quilt. In a wiry sort of way she reminded me of my grandmother. She smiled at me but didn't say a word.

While Mr. Keyholian squeezed the accordion part of the message sender, I peered out of the keyhole to see what was going on. By moving from one side of the apartment to the other, I could see out both sides of the door. Both views were pretty miserable. One side was swarming with rats. On the other side, the munyateeka scuttled around while Heads-or-Tails patrolled in his bat cruiser. He landed alongside the spider monster, climbed out and bounced on his pogo-stick tail to a hologram of the princess, which had appeared on the wall.

She snarled. "Find him, you idiot."

"Maybe the rats got him," said the boar without a body.

"He's still alive," hissed the Princess. "I can feel it in my bones." She growled at the boar. "If you don't find him, I'll strip you of all your groupie privileges."

"No! Not that!" squealed the pig. "Anything but that." He hopped back in his spacecraft and kept searching.

I sat down on the couch alongside Mrs. Keyholian, tapping my hands on a table, my feet on the floor. I was antsy. All this waiting was killing me. I had a city to clean, a planet to save. It was 7:59 p.m. I had to get moving. I had to get back to my team. Only maybe they didn't want me back. And who could blame them?

Key-wee whipped out a paper bag and started munching on some candy.

Her mother frowned. "Dear, it's bad manners not to share with our guest."

Key-wee reluctantly tossed me a piece.

"What is it?" I asked.

"A candy key," said the girl. "They're delicious."

I took a bite. It almost cracked my tooth. "That's OK. I'm not hungry right now." I stuck it in my pocket. "I'll save it for later."

"Good idea," said Mrs. Keyholian.

"Remember this, Giles," said Mr. Keyholian. "If a door can't be unlocked, try the keyhole inside the keyhole."

I had no idea what he was talking about. I was hardly listening. All I could think about was the cement wasteland and the hairy cages and my flyplane trapped inside the munyateeka's belly. When you have a cutting edge vehicle and it gets taken away from you, it's a major drag.

Mr. Keyholian kept on squeezing and typing and huffing

and puffing on the old-school message sender. The darn thing must've worked because five minutes later Tula showed up.

"Welcome, Tula," said Mr. and Mrs. Keyholian in unison.

"Thank you, Keyholians." Tula gave me a big hug. "Giles, I was so worried about you."

I never had a cute girl worried about me before. It was so cool!

Then my heart sank. "DubDub got eaten by a munyateeka."

"Not for long." Tula grabbed her suitcase. She paused. "Oh, that's right, I forgot. You don't want my help. You want to do it all by yourself. I'll just leave you here. Bye, Giles." She pressed the button on her briefcase and disappeared.

"Wait," I screamed. "Tula, come back."

She popped out from behind the lock mechanism, grinning. "Just kidding."

"Ha-ha. She got you," said Key-wee, laughing in my face. "Ha-ha."

I felt like throwing my candy key at her head.

"Listen, Tula," I said. "I'm really sorry about what I said before."

"It's OK, Giles. I forgive you."

When a sky girl forgives you, it's a great feeling.

Tula turned to the Keyholians. "Thank you for everything."

Mr. Keyholian bowed.

"Hey Giles." It was the Keyhole Grandma, speaking for the first time.

I walked over by the little loft and peered up. "Yes?"

She smiled down at me. "*Stewarding* means 'to take care of something.'"

"Oh," I said. "Is that what it means?"

As soon as we climbed down the rope ladder, Tula handed me a brand-new S/U and I returned us to our normal size.

The bat cruiser swooped down on Tula, laser blazing. She deflected the deadly beam with her briefcase. It ricocheted off the wall and blew up the bat cruiser.

Heads-or-Tails ejected himself before being incinerated. He tried to flee on his pogo stick but Tula threw open her briefcase and the squealing pig got sucked into it.

Chuckling, she let me peer inside the briefcase. His head was mounted on the wall of her office.

"You can't mount me on your wall," he protested. "I'm not dead."

"Don't tempt me," Tula said.

The boar shut up.

She calmly closed the briefcase and turned her attention to the munyateeka. Without taking her eyes off it, she reached down and removed the word *kindness* from the side of her briefcase. (It was part of her law firm's motto, remember?) When the monster tried to whip her with its gnarly tail, she nimbly stepped aside and tossed the word into its mouth. The monster swallowed the word *kindness* and began to choke. It gagged. It wheezed. It finally spat it out.

The word *kindness* somersaulted through the air back onto Tula's briefcase. The gatorantula's indigestion problem wasn't finished yet. It spat out everything else in its stomach, which included half a dozen rats and a pair of orange aliens who looked like twins.

"I sure do appreciate that," said the male twin, straightening his top hat, wiping the gatorantula gunk off his tuxedo.

"Can you please give us the coordinates of the nearest intergalactic transport?" said the female twin, wiping the gunk off her satin dress. "We have to get back to the ball."

"Go down that passageway for a mile and a half and make a left," Tula said.

"Thank you."

They wandered off.

The gatorantula let out a deep, deafening reptilian screech of agony. Something was still lodged in its throat. Stomach heaving, hairy legs wobbling, it burped and the final thing came spewing out. It was DubDub!

The flyplane flew in merry circles around my head, landing on my shoulder.

"Let's get going, Giles," Tula said. "We still have a city to clean."

"Hold on a second," I said. "Are you calm and focused? Because I don't feel like landing in a chicken coop again."

"Yes, Giles. I'm calm and focused."

"Good. At least one of us is. I'm totally freaking out."

She pressed the button on her briefcase, and we disappeared.

CHAPTER TWENTY-THREE

IT WAS 8:31P.M. We had three hours and twenty-nine minutes to finish cleaning Manhattan. We were all gathered in the living room, going over our last-minute strategy.

"OK," Bobby said, pacing back and forth. "We lost some time. But we can still pull this off. We just need to stay focused."

For me, that was harder than fighting off a munyateeka.

"I'm going to perform a magic spell so we all stay focused." Nikki closed her eyes and waved her hands in the air. "HOCUS FOCUS!"

I shared the couch with an octopus cloudfish, tentacles resting on my shoulders. Toshi hung out on the floor with Stanley and Big Daddy.

Tula left for half an hour. She got summoned to the Halls of Universal Justice on urgent business again. Maybe that was a good thing. Then she wouldn't see me mess up.

"How much more paper do the droids need to collect?" Toshi asked. "I can't wait to see them turn into trees."

"I'll go check on their numbers," Bobby said, hurrying down the hall into command and control.

While he was gone, the doorbell rang.

Toshi herded Stanley and the cloudfish into the kitchen. I answered the door.

It was the super.

"Listen, we're really busy right now," I told him.

"Hold your horses. I got something for your sister." He pulled a violin out of a sack. "I found it in a junkyard." He handed it to Nikki. "I might be willing to sell it." He rubbed his hands together greedily. "For the right price."

Nikki examined the violin. "Wow! It's a Stradivarius."

"What's that?" asked the super.

Nikki's mouth hit the floor. "You don't know what a Stradivarius is?"

Even I knew what a Stradivarius was. The Rolls-Royce of violins. The supreme musical instrument.

"Never heard of it," said the super.

"Um . . . it's the Walmart brand," Nikki said.

"Walmart makes violins?"

"Yep. They're called Stradivarius."

"All right then. Give me five bucks for it."

"Five bucks for a Stradivarius?" I said. "That's a rip-off."

The super scratched his head. "All right. Three bucks. But I ain't going any lower than that."

"It's a deal." Nikki ran off and came back with three bucks.

The super handed her the violin, snatched the money and took off.

Boy, was it ever fun to rip off the super.

"I'm going to play *The Music of the Spheres* with a Stradivarius," Nikki said, running into her bedroom. "There's no way we can fail the test now."

I needed fuel, so I made myself a grilled cheese.

Just as I was about to take a bite, Bobby hollered, "GILES, GET IN HERE!"

I raced into command and control. Bobby grimaced at an image on the ceiling. It was the super, up on the roof of our building. He was . . . he was peeling off his skin, removing it like a pair of pajamas. It wasn't the super. It was Jerry, boarding his spaceship.

"NIKKI," I yelled, running into her room. "DON'T PLAY THAT VIOLIN!"

It was too late. Her bow was already moving along the strings.

I grabbed the violin from her.

"Giles, what are you doing?" she said.

Toshi burst into the bedroom. "Giles, Big Daddy just collapsed."

In the living room, Big Daddy crawled along the floor, wheezing like a dying man. "Big Daddy doesn't feel so well," he groaned.

A minute later, in command and control, we watched one thousand droids collapse, one by one, onto the sidewalk.

"What's going on?" Nikki said.

"This isn't a Stradivarius," I told her.

"No, it's not," Tula said, striding into the room, taking the violin from me.

"Then what is it?" Nikki said.

"It's a Destructivarius," Tula said.

She hurled it against the wall. It smashed into dozens of pieces. Each piece turned into a scorpion. Nikki screamed. The scorpions had wings. They fluttered around the room like dragonflies, flying in formation in the shape of a violin. They poured out the window into the darkness.

"The sound it creates is deadly black magic," Tula said.

"It alone can neutralize the healing power of *The Music of the Spheres.*"

"And I just played a solo with it," Nikki said.

"Look," Bobby said.

Gruesome images flashed across the ceiling. A witch was playing the trumpet on top of the Plaza Hotel. An ogre banged a gong in the Meatpacking District. Ghoulish creatures were playing musical instruments all over Manhattan.

"Who are they?" asked Toshi.

"The Orchestra of Doom," Tula said. "The princess must've hired them."

"It sounds like the kind of stuff she'd have on her iPod," I said.

We went back into the living room to check on Big Daddy. He rolled around the floor, writhing in pain.

Nikki sobbed. "I killed Big Daddy."

The android weakly took hold of Nikki's hand. "Big Daddy isn't dead yet, Nikki."

"Isn't there anything you can do, Tula?" Bobby asked.

Tula knelt down over the fallen droid. "He has been short circuited. Only a Destructivarius could penetrate the firewall that protects each android's software. I do not have the technical expertise for this kind of repair. But I know someone who does."

"Dr. Sprinkles," I said.

"That's right, Giles. I need to go talk to her."

"Hurry back," I said before she vanished.

All we could do was wait. I spent an endless hour in command and control. All four screens showed the same dreadful thing. Androids slumped on park benches, crouched on curbs, paralyzed, short circuited, waiting for us to rescue them.

I moved restlessly up and down the hallway.

"Giles, have you seen the cloudfish?" Toshi asked from the living room.

"No," I replied. "Ask Nikki. They love her. She'll know where they are."

Nikki said she hadn't seen them in a while.

"How can thousands of cloudfish suddenly vanish?" Toshi said.

Our entire team was falling apart. I raced around the apartment, throwing open closets, peering under beds, searching for cloudfish. I didn't find a single one but I did catch a glimpse of Tula in my parents' bedroom, speaking in a hushed tone to Bobby when she was supposed to be with Dr. Sprinkles.

The door was open a crack. I crept over and eavesdropped.

"Giles never should've let Nikki play that violin," Tula said. "All he does is make mistakes."

I almost fainted like Big Daddy. She blamed me for the Destructivarius. It wasn't my fault, was it? Then again, maybe it was. When your name is Giles, you pretty much take the blame for everything.

Tula went on slamming me. "He should've been able to spot Jerry's disguise. You would've, Bobby. You're so amazing."

"We need to stay calm and figure out a new course of action," Bobby said.

"I know you'll come up with a solution," Tula said. She stared at him for a minute or two. Just the look in her eye, she told him she had a crush on him. She didn't actually say it but my imagination heard it loud and clear. I heard her heart talking. It kept blabbing and blabbing. I felt like screaming,

"Your heart has a really big mouth, Tula. I sure wish it would shut up."

Then she reached over and kissed him. My brother was making out with my girlfriend.

I crept away before I threw up.

In the kitchen Toshi saw me sulking and slapped me on the back. "Dude, what's wrong?"

"Nothing. My girlfriend is in my mom and dad's room making out with Bobby. No big deal. I'll be fine."

"That really sucks," said the parking meter.

I should've guessed. Tula had a crush on Bobby. Just like every other girl on this planet.

Big Daddy was curled up on the kitchen floor. "Sorry, Giles," he mumbled.

Why did I ever get my hopes up? How could I expect a pretty lawyer to go out with a big chocolate eyeball?

"I'm glad I'm too young to like boys," Nikki said. "Liking boys is like liking trouble."

Bobby sauntered into the kitchen. Before he could open the fridge, I attacked. I caught him off guard, punched him in the nose, knocked him to the ground, wrapped my hands around his throat and squeezed and squeezed while Nikki and Toshi tried to pull me off.

"YOU STOLE MY GIRLFRIEND! I'M GOING TO KILL YOU!"

"Giles, *she* kissed *me*!" Bobby said choked out.

"Giles, STOP," Nikki screamed.

They pulled me off. Blood gurgled from his nose. King Goodie-Goodie was bleeding. I was so happy I can't put it into words.

"I'm officially removing you from this quest," I told him.

"Fine," he said, pressing a wet napkin to his nose.

"I wish the Kundabons would come get you," I said. "If there are any Kundabons out there, please take my brother. You can't have my planet, but take my brother, please." I waved my arms maniacally in the air, pointing at the traitor. "Look, he escaped from Desoleen. He escaped. Are you going to let him get away with that?"

There was an eerie silence, broken by a distant howl. Suddenly a Kundabon dropped from the ceiling. Nikki shrieked. It all happened in a horrible instant. The monster grabbed Bobby, stuffed him in its hairy cage and slammed the door shut.

"I was just kidding," I cried. "I didn't mean it." I grabbed one of its albino wings and tried to tear it off. "Let him go!!"

With a flick of its wing, the Kundabon sent me hurtling across the room. Toshi tried the same thing and got pile-driven into the floor. Stanley fired a barrage of quarters. The monster just gave a ghoulish chuckle.

I leaped to my feet and threw myself at the cage, trying to pry open the hairy door while my brother rose helplessly toward the ceiling, trapped behind those bony bars, gripping them with both hands and shaking them in vain, until finally, they were gone.

"He went right through the ceiling," Toshi said in amazement. "Look. They didn't even make a hole."

He was right. The ceiling looked perfectly normal, as if nothing had happened.

"Maybe it didn't happen," Nikki said. "Maybe we're all dreaming."

"We all can't have the same dream, Nikki," I said.

Tula sauntered into the room.

I gritted my teeth. "It's all your fault."

She smirked.

"He wasn't allowed to take Bobby. Was he, Tula?" Toshi asked. "We haven't failed the test yet."

"Giles accused Bobby of escaping from Desoleen," Tula said. "Do you honestly think a Kundabon would let that slide?"

"But we haven't failed the test," Toshi repeated.

"Tula, you cheated on me," I said. "I hate your guts."

"Don't be such a sore loser, Giles," she said.

"Hey, Tula," Toshi said. "whose side are you on?"

She had a nasty cut on her shoulder. She tried to cover it with her hand but it was too big to conceal, a giant gash, growing and spreading from her shoulder all the way down to her forearm, the whole time getting wider and wider. The bizarre thing was, no blood spurted out. If I had a cut half that size, I'd be sprawled out in the ER.

A tiny green dagger emerged from the incision. The pirate tattoo poked his head out. He crawled out with a guilty look on his face.

Petulance glared at him. "You idiot, you ruined my disguise. Why did I ever get a pirate tattoo? I should've gotten a three-headed dragon. It would've been smart enough not to blow my cover." She peeled off her Tula disguise and patted her pirate forgivingly on the head. "He doesn't like to be covered up. He finds it very insulting."

The pirate nodded in agreement and took a swig of rum.

She gazed with bright eyes at the blood on my hand. "See, Giles. You are on my team after all."

I grabbed a frying pan off the stove and threw it at her. Just as it was about to collide with her head, she turned to ash and blew out the window.

Her snotty voice rang out from the shadows. "I'm going to spray paint graffiti on the Sistine Chapel."

I couldn't believe it. I got tricked by another lame disguise. She didn't have her briefcase. Tula never went anywhere without her briefcase. How could I have overlooked that?

"Now what do we do?" asked Toshi.

"I'm going after the Kundabon," I said.

"I'm coming with you," Toshi said.

"I hate to bring this up, guys," said Stanley. "But the fate of humankind is at stake here. I say you get focused on the quest."

"And leave Bobby in a cage? No way," I said.

I had summoned the Kundabon. Now I had to rescue Bobby. It might've been easier to do if the real Tula was by my side but I was too ashamed to contact her. How could I ever think she would cheat on me? She was the most honest girl in the galaxy.

"If you don't clean up New York, you'll all end up on Desoleen," the parking meter reminded us.

"Like I could forget that," I said.

"I want my brother back," Nikki pleaded.

"Don't worry, Nikki, I'll bring him back," I said.

I shrank down. So did Toshi. We hopped in our flyplanes and flew off into battle.

CHAPTER TWENTY-FOUR

I SOARED OVER CENTRAL PARK, hating myself. If anyone belonged in a cage it was me. I veered right at the Bethesda Fountain, heading toward the East River. I had no idea where I was going, no idea where to look.

Giles, the Kundabon is not allowed to remove Bobby from the island of Manhattan.

That's good news, DubDub.

Your species has not failed the test yet.

No thanks to me, DubDub.

The monster has to wait until midnight. As hideous as they may seem, Kundabons do obey the law.

You know what law I obey, DubDub? Always act like an idiot. That is the golden rule of Giles.

Toshi broke in over my intercom. "Hey Giles. I think Superfly located the Kundabon."

I met up with him on Lexington Avenue.

"He's in that building over there," Toshi said. "In apartment Five-B."

We darted through an open window. I landed on a coffee table while Toshi set down on the DVD player. A man and a woman sat on the couch. The Kundabon was nowhere to be seen.

DubDub opened a compartment below his gas gauge. A pair of goggles popped out.

Put these KGs on, Giles.

What are KGs, DubDub?

Kundabon goggles. They will enable you to see the Kundabon even when it has made itself invisible to rest of your species.

I put them on.

There was the Kundabon, hanging from a light fixture in the center of the room. Bobby also dangled from the ceiling, in the hairy cage, screaming at the man and woman.

Why can't they hear him, DubDub?

The Kundabon has the power to make its cage undetectable to all the senses.

I couldn't hear my brother either.

"What's our plan, Giles?" Toshi asked over the intercom.

Before I could answer him, the lady on the couch tried to crush me with a fly swatter.

"Thanks a lot, lady," I felt like saying. "I'm trying to save the planet and you nail me with a fly swatter. Now that's what I call gratitude."

The guy went after me with a rolled up newspaper. "Die, sucker," he growled.

For a moment I realized how tough it was to be a fly. I

had nothing against flies in general. Flies just do what they have to do. They bother people and cling to poop. No one asked the flies, "Do you want to cling to poop?" They never had a choice. They didn't say, "Oh yeah, sure. Give us that job."

The lady put down the swatter and turned to the guy. "It just doesn't make sense. Why would you want a divorce?"

"I want a new life for myself," he said.

She sobbed hysterically. I almost wished I'd let her swat me.

It's not a coincidence that the Kundabon entered this room, Giles.

Why's that, DubDub?

Kundabons are drawn to misery.

The woman bawled her head off. "But I still love you," she said.

The Kundabon eyed her falling tears ravenously. Licking its lips, the creature unrolled a grotesque white tongue all the way down to her cheek and lapped up a tear.

The woman cringed in disgust and confusion. "Something just licked me."

"You're hallucinating," said the man, staring blankly at the television.

"We have to get rid of these people before we launch our attack," I told Toshi. "Otherwise they could get hurt."

I commanded DubDub to pick up the leather recliner and make it hover in midair.

"THIS APARTMENT IS HAUNTED!" I bellowed over the loudspeaker. "LEAVE RIGHT NOW! YOU'RE REALLY ANNOYING ME!"

They ran out, screaming.

Now it was just me, Toshi and the Kundabon.

"OK, Toshi," I said. "Let's do it."

The Kundabon wasn't even paying any attention to us. With his cage full, he seemed bloated, like a python that just swallowed a rabbit. He burped, a sleepy grin crawling across his foul face. You would've thought he just won the lottery.

I couldn't wait to see the look on the monster's face after I shrunk Bobby down and whisked him away. My big brother was about to become the first rabbit ever stolen from a python's belly.

Rabbits would love me. I was about to become a legend in the rabbit community. If I ever grew lettuce, they'd leave it alone.

DubDub furtively entered the cage. We flew into the cave of Bobby's right ear. I whispered, "Bobby, it's me. I'm in your ear in the flyplane. Act normal. I don't want the Kundabon knowing I'm here. I'm going to shrink you down then we'll get out of here."

We glided out of his ear and settled on his shoulder.

I commanded my S/U to shrink Bobby down.

Nothing happened. I tried again. And again. And again. Bobby didn't shrink.

Hey, DubDub, why isn't my S/U working? It's brand-new.

A Kundabon's cage is a universe unto its own, Giles. It emits an ultraviolet radiation that is blocking the S/Us signal.

Why did I even ask? Nothing works inside a Kundabon's cage. Nothing except your panic button. And let me tell you something. Mine was working real good.

As if that wasn't bad enough, DubDub accidentally brushed up against one of the stiff white hairs protruding from the bony bars, tripping some kind of sensor. These whiskers, and there were thousands of them, began billowing back and forth, as if they were coming to life.

We flew back into Bobby's ear. "Bobby," I whispered, "the S/U won't work on you as long as you're inside the cage. So I'm going to blast open the door. You hop out. Then I'll shrink you down and we'll leave this dump."

When we flew out of the cage, one of the whiskers tried to lasso us but DubDub dodged it.

Toshi and I lined up side by side and upside down on the ceiling, ten feet away from the Kundabon.

"Take off his head, Toshi," I said. "Then I'll blast the door."

"Got it," Toshi replied.

"On three. One, two, three . . ."

Toshi fired his laser. The monster's head split in half to dodge the beam and glued itself back together.

I had to admit. It was rather impressive.

The monster laughed at us and escaped through the ceiling.

That didn't go too well, DubDub.

Giles, we need the cloudfish. Cloudfish can be extremely pesky to a Kundabon.

I contacted Nikki back at command and control. She was running things now that Bobby was temporarily out of the picture.

"Nikki, send in the cloudfish."

"I still can't find them, Giles."

"Toshi," I said, "see if you can track down the cloudfish. I'm going after the Kundabon."

"Got it, dude," Toshi said.

Nikki sent me some disturbing video footage from an alien news channel. A two-headed reporter was interviewing some purple aliens who came from the same planet as Princess Petulance.

"Are you excited about moving to Earth?" the reporter asked.

"We can't wait," said a purple guy, who was sticking his head out of an alien U-Haul star cruiser.

"It's a new beginning for us," his wife said in the passenger's seat.

"Well, it won't be long now," said the reporter. "It's almost midnight."

The couple smiled for the camera. They were part of a convoy of thousands of U-Haul star cruisers and gargantuan flying moving vans. One van had ACME MOVING COMPANY painted on the side. Another van had STARVING STUDENT MARTIAN MOVERS. They were all waiting in a parking lot behind the moon.

The news coverage switched to Desoleen, where a different alien reporter was standing on the concrete wasteland, holding a microphone. "The humans will be arriving tomorrow morning. We will be here to interview them as part of our continuing coverage of the eviction process."

I turned off my video monitor. I couldn't stand to see anymore.

Why didn't Bobby ever tell me about that alien news channel? He must've watched it from command and control. Maybe he didn't want to freak me out. He was protecting me. My big brother was protecting me. How did I pay him back? By putting him in a hairy cage.

I caught up with the Kundabon high above Times Square, its awful albino face illuminated by the glow of countless neon signs. Sensing my presence, it flapped its wings, diving down through the roof of a Broadway theater. Because Bobby was a captive inside the cage, he too was able to pass unharmed right through buildings, while I had to fly through an air vent in order to enter the theater.

How come you can't go through walls, DubDub?

I don't know, Giles. Some of the newer flyplane models have that feature. If you want, you can trade me in for a newer model.

I'd never trade you in, DubDub.

Thank you, Giles.

The theater was packed with people applauding a musical called *Creepy Creatures*. The Kundabon landed in the middle of the stage alongside a singing werewolf. People gasped and pointed. The Kundabon took a bow. The werewolf didn't appreciate this at all.

They can see the Kundabon, DubDub. Even without KGs. Why did it reveal itself to them?

Because he is a ham, Giles. He loves attention.

But they'll call the police. They'll bring in the air force and the marines. The Kundabon doesn't want to deal with all that, does he?

The audience doesn't think he's real, Giles. Look. They think he's part of the show. The Kundabon knows this. They're highly intelligent creatures.

The curtain came down for intermission. I flew backstage. Half a dozen jealous actors surrounded the Kundabon.

The vampire was heartbroken. "He's got a better costume than me."

"Who designed your costume?" asked the werewolf suspiciously.

"The Dark Lord of the Universe," hissed the Kundabon.

"Could you give me his card?" inquired the vampire.

Because there were so many people around, I couldn't fire any artillery at the Kundabon and run the risk of hurting someone. I had to be patient. It wasn't easy. When your brother is trapped in a hairy cage and your species is about to get evicted and it's all your fault, you kind of want to get things moving.

Even DubDub was getting antsy.

Giles, we must have the cloudfish. Without them we are at the mercy of this monster.

I contacted Toshi. "Any luck finding the cloudfish?"

"My radar is showing something out over Long Island Sound," Toshi said. "I'm going to investigate."

When the curtain came back up, the mummy elbowed the Kundabon in the ribs. "Hey, dude, this is my scene."

"Is that so?" the Kundabon replied, picking up the mummy like a rag doll and tossing him into the balcony.

The crowd cheered.

The Kundabon climbed down into the audience, crawling on all fours up the aisle, dragging Bobby.

Everyone in the theater could see my frantic brother inside the hairy cage.

"Help!" he pleaded. "Get me out of here!"

The audience laughed at him.

"We're not part of the show!" Bobby cried.

"Check out his eyelids," someone said, snapping the monster's photograph. "God, are they cool."

The Kundabon's red, triangle-shaped eyes had three ghost white lids, which all met over the black slit of his pupil when he blinked.

"You're so lifelike," a woman wearing a neck brace said.

"He's a real monster," Bobby said.

"That kid is a lousy actor," someone snorted.

"I'm not an actor." Bobby reached out his hands toward a boy in the back. "If you get me out of here, I'll give you a free copy of my book. It's called *How to Get Your Homework Done*. Dude, you'll never fail another exam."

The monster soared up through the roof and was gone.

The crowd went berserk.

"Did you see that? It went right through the ceiling!"

"These are the coolest special effects I've ever seen!"

I chased the Kundabon across the city.

Down below us, on almost every block, androids were slumped on park benches, too weak to get up and clean the city, unable to take the final steps to transform themselves into trees.

It was almost ten o'clock. Only two hours left.

I saw something suspicious on a side street in Gramercy Park and flew down to investigate.

A man and woman were unloading a U-Haul in the moonlight. Glancing over her shoulder to make sure no one was watching, the woman picked up a piano by herself and placed it on the curb.

I flicked on my loudspeaker and tried to sound like a cop, "Boy, you sure are strong. Aren't you, lady?"

The woman almost fainted from shock. She flashed a worried smile. "It's all that Pilates."

The husband peered underneath the truck, trying to figure out where the voice was coming from.

"What are you two up to?" I said.

"Nothing, officer," said the woman. "We're just moving into our new apartment. We're so excited to be living in Gramercy Park."

"It's a dream come true," the man added.

"What planet are you from?" I said.

"Uh . . . Earth," the man mumbled.

"Sure you are."

Firing a precise laser, DubDub peeled off the skin on the man's left hand. A purple claw slipped out. The man tried desperately to hide it in his coat pocket.

"You're not allowed to move in yet," I said. "The humans have not been evicted. I'm a marshal from the Halls of Universal Justice. Do you want me to place you under arrest?"

The woman elbowed her husband. "I told you we should've waited."

"Yeah, but if we waited all the prime real estate will get gobbled up. Do you want to end up in Yonkers?"

"I'd rather be in Yonkers than a maximum-security intergalactic prison!" I yelled.

"That's a very good point, officer. We're leaving right away."

They hopped in the van and vanished through an envelope in space.

The Kundabon was watching from a rooftop across the street.

I followed it helplessly into the grand ballroom of a hotel, where a wedding reception was taking place. Hanging from a chandelier above the dance floor, unnoticed by all the gyrating people, he unrolled his endless tongue toward the mother of the bride, licking a tear off her cheek.

He spat it out.

Why did he spit out the tear, DubDub?

It was a happy tear, Giles. Happy tears burn a hole in a Kundabon's tongue like acid.

I flew into my brother's ear and tried to comfort him. "Hey, Bobby, it won't be much longer. I give you my word."

Toshi's voice buzzed over my intercom. "Giles, I found the cloudfish."

"Way to go, Toshi. Only cloudfish can take down a Kundabon."

"I don't think they can take down anyone, Giles."

"What do you mean?"

"I mean the cloudfish are being taken down."

CHAPTER TWENTY-FIVE

DUBDUB FLICKED ON my monitor, allowing Toshi to transmit video footage. Thousands of cloudfish were gathered out over the Long Island Sound, diving one after another like pelicans into the ocean. None of them came back out of the water. It was pretty spooky.

"It looks like they're drowning, Toshi. Why do they keep diving in?"

"The lobster cloudfish is trapped at the bottom of the sea. The princess put it there. She's got some kind of high-tech lobster trap. The other cloudfish are trying to rescue it."

A school of dolphin cloudfish plunged into the murky water.

DubDub interrupted my talk with Toshi.

This is a very disturbing development, Giles. Cloudfish can't swim. They are allergic to water. The only way to kill a cloudfish is by drowning it. It is the ultimate paradox.

I had no idea what that meant, but I couldn't stop to find out.

Is there anything Toshi can do, DubDub?

He must dive down to the bottom of the sea and free the lobster cloudfish. His flyplane has submarine capability. It is armed with torpedoes.

"OK, Toshi," I said, still inside my brother's ear. "I'm sure Superfly told you what to do. Go dive down and rescue the lobster."

"There's one big problem, Giles."

"What's that, Toshi?"

"I can't swim."

"Dude, you're going to be in a submarine. You don't have to swim."

"Dude, you don't understand. Just being near water freaks me out."

"Dude, get your butt into the ocean right now. I can't believe I'm having this conversation."

"What about sharks?" Toshi asked.

"DUDE, YOU'RE THE SIZE OF A HOUSEFLY. DO YOU THINK A GREAT WHITE SHARK IS GOING TO WASTE ITS TIME ON YOU?"

Toshi's voice broke up. The line went dead.

We will get better reception outside the Kundabon's cage, Giles.

OK, DubDub.

We flew out of Bobby's ear.

Do the cloudfish know they'll drown if they dive in, Dub-Dub?

Yes, Giles. The cloudfish would prefer to all die in a rescue effort than to let one of their own perish. It is the nature of cloudfish.

It is the nature of a Kundabon to not let you leave its cage. When we tried to leave the cage by zipping in between the hairy bars, the whiskers grabbed DubDub, wrapping around his wings. DubDub fired a laser at them, trying to unmummify his wings. For each whisker we removed, a dozen more slithered up from the bony bars.

"Toshi, I'm trapped," I yelled over the intercom.

Could he hear me? What if . . . what if he was stabbing me in the back? We removed the black butterfly, right? But what if it planted an egg?

I tried not to believe it. I tried to have faith.

High above Saint Patrick's Cathedral, DubDub sat motionless in the center of the cage, tangled up in whiskers. Luckily the belligerent bristles had yet to penetrate the cockpit. Like cobras, they eyed me ravenously, pressing their faces up against the glass dome of the cockpit, trying to find a way in. They were so sneaky and slippery and slimy, they found a crack in the glass where there wasn't a crack. Somehow they slithered right through the glass into the cockpit, swarming all over me, coiling around my throat. I couldn't fend them off. I was slowly suffocating.

I began to hallucinate. I saw Toshi soaring over Fifth Avenue with an army of cloudfish, coming to the rescue.

The Kundabon panicked when it saw the cloudfish. It took off, heading west, in the direction of the George Washington Bridge. The grip around my throat seemed to loosen, as if the whiskers were weakened by the monster's fear.

Wait. This wasn't a dream. It really was Toshi! He must've rescued the lobster!

A school of dolphin cloudfish formed a rainbow high above the George Washington Bridge. Moonlit rainbows have an otherworldly luster. The Kundabon flew into it, grimacing as if it had just been scalded. If you're a Kundabon, a rainbow is a big problem. A rainbow is to a Kundabon what a crucifix is to a vampire. He kept brushing up against bits of iridescense in the night sky. Each time it happened the whiskers weakened until finally DubDub broke free and flew out of the cage, spinning figure eights over a tugboat on the Hudson River.

"Toshi, can you hear me?"

"I sure can, dude," he said, pulling up alongside me in Superfly.

"You did it, Toshi. You came through in the clutch."

"We still need to free your brother."

This was true.

A pair of fully armed flyplanes zeroed in on the George Washington Bridge. The monster perched on a suspension cable, trying to catch its breath. Cloudfish surrounded it, swimming through the air in frantic circles. More cloudfish waited in ambush behind the tollbooth on the Jersey side. The monster had nowhere to go.

The door on the Kundabon's cage had a keyhole.

Do Keyholians live in there, DubDub?

No, Giles. Nothing can live in there.

Digging into my pocket, I pulled out the candy key given to me by Key-wee. It couldn't hurt to try. While traffic streamed back and forth across the bridge only a few feet away, I flew into the keyhole on the monster's hairy cage. Another much smaller keyhole existed inside it, just as Mr. Keyholian predicted. Smart guy. It was just big enough to fit the candy key. The door on the cage opened. It made the loudest weirdest creaking sound you've ever heard. If you took the sound of every rusty door opening in the history of the world and put them together, that's about what it sounded like.

"Hey, Kundabon," I yelled over the loudspeaker. "You need to oil those hinges, you creep."

It was so loud it made the George Washington Bridge sway. Cars swerved and skidded.

Bobby stepped out of the cage, tottering on the edge, peering at the water one thousand feet down. He hurled himself forward, so desperate to escape he forgot all about the danger of jumping. If I hadn't come soaring by in my flyplane, he would've plunged to his death in the Hudson River. I shrank him down in midair and popped open the hatch in my copilot's seat. He landed safely inside it.

"What's up, Bobby?" I said.

"Not much. How's it going, Giles?"

The Kundabon couldn't believe it. He was more shocked than I had been when I saw Tula kiss Bobby. He just stared at his empty cage. It blew his evil mind. He burst out crying. The big hairy monster started bawling. Tears gushed out, a streaming waterfall cascading into the Hudson River.

Giles, those are all the tears he ever licked since the beginning of time. He is required by Kundabon law to release them if someone escapes from his cage.

Cool, DubDub!

Defeating a Kundabon is one of life's great pleasures. But it was 10:50 p.m. The city still wasn't clean.

We were in big trouble.

CHAPTER TWENTY-SIX

THE REAL TULA sat at our kitchen table with a glum look on her face. "I was hoping Dr. Sprinkles would be able to repair the androids. Unfortunately Dr. Sprinkles is no position to be helping anyone."

"Why not?" I said, bouncing frantically around the room, way too nervous to sit down.

"She's in a dungeon on Venus."

"A dungeon?" Bobby said. "What happened?"

"She was walking past a yoga studio. There were a bunch of shoes just sitting there, since people take off their shoes before doing yoga. Dr. Sprinkles saw a pair of sandals she liked and stole them. It turns out they belonged to the queen."

"What is wrong with that lady?" I said. "Why is she so into shoes?"

"It will take me at least a week to get her released from prison," Tula said.

"We'll all be hanging out on Desoleen by then," Toshi said.

I glanced at the clock, 11:02. I threw open the freezer and slammed it shut. "That's it," I said, punching the refrigerator door. "I don't care what anyone says. I'm going to Jersey and I'm stealing all their trees."

"I'm with you, Giles," Toshi said.

"I agree," Bobby said. "We'll shrink them down and re-plant them in Central Park."

Tula jumped up from the table, cornered me by the microwave and unleashed a furious whisper: "I'd never go out with a tree stealer."

She plopped back down at the table.

I punched Toshi in the arm. "Toshi, how many times do I have to tell you? We're not stealing any trees."

"Dude, it was your idea," he said.

"Can't you do some magic with your briefcase, Tula?" Nikki said.

"I'd get charged with tampering, Nikki," Tula explained. "That's a serious offense. You humans would get evicted automatically."

"Scratch that," Toshi said.

I hovered over the sink, tapping a spoon insanely on the faucet, staring out the window. Down below, a boy picked up a candy wrapper off the street and handed it to an ailing street cleaner sprawled out on a park bench. The android tossed it feebly into his trash can and thanked the kid. I recognized the kid. It was the nerd from the community garden, the one who picked up the fridge by himself.

On the other side of the street, two other kids were fishing newspapers out of the gutter and stuffing them in the trash can of a lady street cleaner. Three other kids on the next block were collecting cardboard boxes outside a newsstand and breaking them up.

"Hey, you guys," I said. "Come take a look at this."

Everyone ran to the window.

"Look," I said, "they're out there helping the street cleaners. They don't even know what's at stake." I panicked.

"They are allowed to clean. Aren't they, Tula? This isn't a violation, is it?"

"Of course not," she said. "Children are allowed to clean their planet."

Hands trembling with excitement, I whipped out my smart phone and called Navida. "Kids are out there helping the street cleaners, Navida."

"It's not my fault, Giles. They did it on their own. The cleaners look so exhausted. They were just trying to help. I hope they're not ruining everything."

"Ruining? They're saving the day."

"They are? I thought you said we weren't supposed to bother the street cleaners."

"I had it all wrong. They love to be bothered. There's nothing they love more than when kids bother them. And the best way to bother them is by picking up recyclables and filling up their trash cans. That's their favorite kind of bothering. They'd rather be bothered by that than by getting a million bucks."

"How is a million bucks a bother, Giles?"

I had to think about that for a second. "Well, you've got to open a Swiss bank account. You've got to figure out where you're going to park your Ferrari. Parking a car is a major problem in New York City. That's why everyone takes cabs."

"OK, OK. I get it, Giles."

"Go get recyclables, Navida. Tell everyone to go get them and give them to the street cleaners."

"I'll spread the word."

"Tell them it must be done by midnight."

"Why?" Navida asked. "Is midnight some kind of deadline?"

"I can't say."

"No problem, Giles. I'll tell everyone we need to finish by then because all good kids should be in bed by midnight."

"Now you're talking," I said.

Navida posted it on her blog.

She posted it on Facebook and Twitter.

Within ten minutes, kids were springing into action, rich and poor, swarming out of brownstones and skyscrapers, roaming the streets of Manhattan, snatching up paper and glass and plastic and feeding them to the street cleaners.

Even kids who didn't read Navida's blog found out. (I bet you're wondering how. Aren't you, reader? Well, the Empire State Building is half the size of a child's curiosity.) When children peered out their bedroom windows and saw streets full of kids, they wondered what was going on. They had to go check it out for themselves. When they got down there, they caught the fever. The fever of cleaning, polishing the city until it sparkled like a diamond.

More and more kids got on board. Five dozen became five hundred, five hundred became five thousand. It kept gathering momentum, a beautiful snowball rolling through the heatwave, an unstoppable, unbeatable, unmeltable snowball.

Even Buck the bully, the super's son, was standing by my side, picking up bottles in front of our building. Buck was on my team. How bizarre is that?

Every street, every block was swarming with kids. We halted traffic.

"Why don't you arrest these little punks?" a frustrated cabbie told a cop.

"Why don't I arrest you instead?" said the cop.

We all cheered for the cop. He took off his cap and bowed to us.

Bobby was up in command and control, monitoring the progress of the droids. He relayed the numbers back to me. This enabled me to determine which street cleaners needed more paper and plastic. I alternated between between zipping around in the flyplane, barking out orders over the loud-speaker, and making myself big so I could join the fun and roam the streets with all the kids.

I stepped in front of one kid who was about to stuff something into a trash can. "No, this guy's can is full. Go give the newspaper to that guy over there."

Toshi and Nikki passed out lemonade to everyone while they worked.

Navida barked out orders. "Come on. Keep moving. Midnight's almost here."

Parents didn't know what to think.

"Shouldn't they be in bed?" said one woman.

"Oh, let them have some fun," said her husband.

"Since when did our son think cleaning up was fun?"

"What's come over these kids?" declared another lady.

"They've lost their minds."

"It's all that Twittering."

"They've gone crazy."

"I'm telling you. It's the Twittering."

Senior citizens set up lawn chairs on the sidewalk as if they were watching a parade.

In Times Square, CNN had a giant monitor, one hundred feet tall. Video streamed across it of kids in Boston and Philadelphia cleaning their streets, kids in Chicago, Dallas and L.A. They must've found out through the Internet. Kids were telling kids, not just in America, but all over the world.

"It's a global phenomenon," said a CNN reporter.

Gazing in wonder up at the screen, I watched kids cleaning the streets of Rio de' Janeiro, Buenos Aires, London, Paris, Rome, Berlin, Moscow, Hong Kong, Shanghai, Capetown, Cairo, Tel Aviv.

I was tempted to fly to Shanghai to check it out in person and have an eggroll but I had to stay focused on the quest right here in Manhattan. It was all about staying focused.

"Hocus focus," I repeated to myself. "Hocus focus."

The time was 11:27.

I met up with Tula in a quiet alleyway, shrank us both down and shot up to Harlem in the flyplane to see how things were going.

One Hundred Twenty-fifth Street was immaculate.

We spotted Jerry on a rooftop, all alone, sobbing like a baby. What depressed him appeared to be a slip of paper floating in front of him. He couldn't take his eyes off it. Tears gushed down his striped face.

"Why's Jerry crying, Tula?"

"I filed a complaint with the Universal Real Estate Association, Giles. His license has been suspended."

That sheet of paper hovering in front of him was his real estate license. On other planets, when your license gets suspended, it literally gets suspended in the air. Boy, did that ever put me in a good mood. Then I made a discovery that put me in an even better one.

"Tula, look!"

A tiny leaf sprouted from a street cleaner's forehead. He covered it with a New York Yankees baseball cap.

By 11:45, all the androids had reached their quota. One by one, they limped into Central Park, Madison Square Park, East River Park, taking a last sip of lemonade, vines emerging from their fingertips, waving good-bye as they disappeared into the darkness.

They were ready to turn into trees!

Our entire team, except Navida of course, gathered in command and control to witness the transformation on the giant screens. Bobby flicked a switch so we could see through the cloudfish. But this wasn't some pay-per-view event the rest of the world got to watch. Only those who knew about the test. Tula passed out jars of traffic jam to munch on.

"I can't wait to see roots shoot out of their feet," I said.

"Me too," said Toshi.

"I want to see branches come out of their ears," said Nikki.

This would be by far the coolest thing we ever witnessed on TV. However, when the clock struck midnight, instead of torsos turning into tree trunks, what flashed before our eyes was the diabolical face of Princess Petulance. She hijacked the video signal, broadcasting her purple sneer on all four screens, the tattoo pirate perched on her shoulder.

"Congratulations, Giles," she said. "It looks as if you're about to pass the test. But there's one thing you need to know about me. I'm a sore loser." She peered down at her pirate. "Aren't I?"

The pirate waved his little dagger at us menacingly.

"The tip of the dagger has been dipped in poison, Giles," said the princess, laughing. "Go check on Grandma."

I raced down the hallway, burst into her room and threw on the light.

Grandma was lying in bed, eyes closed, a tiny laceration on her left cheek.

I pressed my ear to her chest. "Her heart's not beating. Why isn't it beating?"

Bobby pushed me out of the way and pressed his ear to her breast. He looked up, tears streaming down his face. "She's dead."

Tula stepped forward and waved her briefcase over Grandma from head to toe.

"Is Grandma dead, Tula?" Nikki cried.

"I'm afraid she is," Tula said.

At that moment, all the excitement of saving the planet shriveled up and disappeared.

"It's all my fault as usual," I said. "I was supposed to take care of her. I promised Grandpa I'd take care of her."

Tula gently took my hand.

I jerked my hand away. "Why did you give me this quest? I already had a quest. To take care of Grandma. To save her from a broken heart. I gave Grandpa my word I'd look after her."

I was bawling harder than the Kundabon that made a waterfall over the George Washington Bridge.

"Isn't there anything you can do, Tula?" Bobby asked.

"There is only one way to counteract this poison," Tula said.

"Tell us how," Nikki pleaded.

"Giles must journey to the source of all life in the universe."

"What place is that?" I asked.

"The Stellar Nursery."

I remembered that creepy thing Bobby showed me, the baby crib floating in deep space. It was about a million miles long, made out of boiling blood red mist, supported by pillars of black fog crackling with lightning.

"I have to go in that thing?" I said. "And do what?"

"According to my briefcase, the poison used on your

grandmother was extracted from the remains of a dead planet. It can only be counteracted by something that helps give birth to planets."

"And what would that be?" Bobby said.

"Star milk."

"Star milk?" I said. "Is there such a thing?"

"There most certainly is. You humans are raised on milk, Giles. So are baby stars. They drink star milk. A drop of it will bring your grandmother back from the dead."

"Then I'm going," I said.

"I must warn you," Tula said, "the Stellar Nursery is the most inhospitable place in the entire universe. There is only a one-in-ten chance you'll survive."

"One in ten?" Bobby said. "No way. I don't like those odds. I'm not sending my kid brother to his death."

"I'm going, Bobby," I said. "I don't care what you think."

"Giles, now that Grandma's gone I'm the oldest. I'm in charge. I'm the head of this household and I forbid you to go."

"Don't you care about Grandma?" I said.

"Of course. But . . ."

"No buts. I'm going."

"I'll go with you," Big Daddy said, leaning against the wall, knees wobbling, standing for the first time in hours, "I'm feeling much better now."

Tula smiled. "You're not ready for the Stellar Nursery, Big Daddy."

"I am," Bobby said. "I'm going with him."

"Bobby," Tula said, "your brother's chances of survival are greater if he flies without a copilot."

Toshi offered to fly alongside me in Superfly but Tula wouldn't allow it. Saving Grandma was my quest.

Five minutes later, Tula and I were alone in the kitchen while I got ready to take off in the flyplane.

She handed me a green vial. "Put the star milk in here."

"Sure thing." I stuffed the vial in my pocket. "Tula, I have a favor to ask."

"Anything, Giles."

"Listen, this is really hard to say but . . . but . . . I don't want to die without ever having kissed a girl. So can we kiss?"

"No."

"Why not?"

"Then you won't die," Tula said. "If you die without ever having kissed a girl, it'll be extremely embarrassing. When you get to heaven they'll all laugh at you. Oh, here comes Giles. He never kissed a girl. Ha-ha."

"Well then, I guess I'd better not die."

She wrapped her arms around me. "You'd better not."

CHAPTER TWENTY-SEVEN

I HOPPED IN THE FLYPLANE.

We need fuel, Giles.

Give me a riddle, DubDub.

If you spill milk on a dictionary, how do you clean it up?

You mop up vowels with paper towels.

Correct, Giles.

We zipped out the window into the summer night, soaring straight up until we broke through the stratosphere and glided through outer space.

Giles, what we are about to attempt is extremely dangerous.

It's a risk I have to take, DubDub.

Giles, the pressure inside the Stellar Nursery is fifty thousand pounds per square inch. That's triple the pressure a deep-sea vessel experiences at the bottom of the ocean. Are you sure you can handle it?

No problem.

Giles, we will have no margin for error.

Me, Giles, commit an error? Come on, DubDub. Get serious.

I may have been acting cocky but I sure didn't feel it. Wiping my forehead with my shirt, I tried to conceal my cold sweat from the flyplane. I didn't want DubDub to think it brought a coward into outer space.

The Stellar Nursery loomed up ahead, shrouded in bloody mist, veined with lightning. We were being sucked into it slowly and DubDub didn't fight the gravitational pull. We kept going toward the black pillars that were light years long.

We descended into the monstrous crib. How could we ever find a measly drop of milk in here? Before I could even begin to worry about that my skin started shriveling. I was impersonating a raisin and it wasn't much fun. How I didn't have a broken neck I'll never know. That's how bad DubDub shook.

I wished I was back in the sewer with the gatorantula. I never thought I'd miss a gatorantula but I sure did miss it now.

We got hammered by stellar winds, thrashed by boiling gases, pummeled by gamma ray bursts. The light was so blinding I could hardly see. It was so bright my vital organs got a suntan. You know it's bright out when you've got to put SPF 45 on your liver and kidneys.

Just in case you didn't know, stars are formed by gravity caving in, collapsing under unendurable pressure. Imagine if a hurricane hit an island that had a volcano on it, and the volcano erupted while the hurricane was still blowing, so now, not only do you have five-hundred-mile-per-hour winds to deal with, you've also got lava coming at you.

That's kind of what I was dealing with. But much worse.

My head couldn't possibly survive this pressure. It was about to explode. I apologized to DubDub for the brain gunk that would soon be splattered all over the control panel.

Do you want to turn back, Giles?

No.

If we go any deeper, you might not survive.

Keep going, DubDub.

Down and down we went into the bright, blazing abyss. I caught sight of an embryonic star through a veil of cosmic dust. A drop of moisture glistened on the rim of its circumstellar disk.

Is that star milk, DubDub?

I'm not sure, Giles. I need to take a closer look.

Suddenly I felt a knifing pain in the center of my chest. My left arm went completely numb. I couldn't breathe.

A kid my age can't have a heart attack, can he, DubDub?

The flyplane didn't answer. It didn't need to. Of course a kid can have a heart attack when he is stupid enough to enter the Stellar Nursery.

We have to turn back, DubDub. I'm having a heart attack.

DubDub kept going.

Didn't you hear what I just said?

The flyplane ignored me.

Why aren't you listening to me, you stupid spaceship?

It remained silent.

I thought I could trust you. I thought you were my friend. I was wrong, wasn't I, DubDub? Wasn't I? You betrayed me.

The pain in my chest got ten times worse. Cold sweat drenched my entire body. I vomited.

DubDub collected a glistening drop off the tip of the fledgling star and shot out of the Stellar Nursery through seething vapors and a golden whirlpool of cosmic dust.

We had escaped into calm black space but the serenity was shattered by the anarchy of cardiac arrest.

As a kid you never think about dying but I sure was thinking about it now.

Two pincers shot out of DubDub's console, gently opened my trembling mouth and dabbed some kind of liquid on my foaming tongue. It tasted like every delicious thing I'd ever sipped. Every butterscotch shake, every hot fudge malt, every can of Mountain Dew, every strawberry-banana-acai smoothie.

The pain in my chest subsided as the joy in my taste buds grew. The trembling and the dizziness and the nausea and the cold sweat vanished.

Not only was I back to normal, I felt fantastic, even better than I did after eating traffic jam. Even better than I did when we rescued Bobby from the Kundabon's cage.

What happened, DubDub?

I gave you some star milk, Giles.

Is there still some left for Grandma?

There's more than enough. I'm sorry I disobeyed you,

Giles. I had no alternative. If we had turned back without gathering the star milk, you would've died.

I sure am glad you disobeyed me, DubDub.

You can trust me, Giles.

I know I can.

A minute later, we were back on Earth, soaring through Grandma's bedroom window.

Tula tenderly opened Grandma's mouth. I poured the liquid from the green vial down her throat.

"That's enough, Giles," Tula said. "We don't want to give her too much."

There was still some star milk left in the vial. I put it in my pocket.

Tula asked everyone but me to go wait out in the living room.

"Giles, you sit here with your grandmother and be patient," she said. She pressed the button on her briefcase and disappeared.

Big Daddy popped his head into the room and whispered, "You went into the Stellar Nursery and survived. You're Big Daddy. From now on I'm Almost Big Daddy. My initials are ABD. That stands for Almost Big Daddy." He quietly shut the door.

I waited all night. At ten in the morning I was still sitting by Grandma's bed. Finally she opened her eyes. It was the greatest thing that ever happened to me.

"Hi, Grandma," I said back. "How are you feeling?"

"I feel great." She sprang out of bed like a ten-year-old.

That star milk is good stuff.

"How long have I been sleeping?" she asked.

"Quite a long time, Grandma."

"How long would that be?"

"Three days."

She burst out laughing. "You're such a kidder."

I followed her into the living room. They were all gone except for Nikki.

Grandma did a cartwheel across the room and gave my little sister a kiss. She paused, scratched her head. "Am I going senile or did I just do a cartwheel?"

"You just did a cartwheel, Grandma," I said.

"Well I'll be . . ."

"It just goes to show the importance of a good night's sleep," Nikki said.

"When I was a child I could cartwheel with the best of 'em," Grandma said, dumbstruck.

"You haven't lost your touch, Grandma," I said.

She grabbed her keys off the kitchen table. "Come on, kids. Let's get some fresh air. The park is calling."

Riding down in the elevator, my stomach started churning. I felt jittery, panicky. I felt doomed. What if the androids didn't turn into trees? Then we would've been evicted at midnight, right? Maybe they were waiting, waiting for me to get my hopes up. Then Bang! Off to Desoleen.

CHAPTER TWENTY-EIGHT

WE STEPPED OUTSIDE into a strangely perfect city. Central Park had been supersized. The trees were taller, thicker, grander. Squirrels in the upper branches were peering down at penthouses. Oaks and maples as tall as redwoods surrounded the Central Park Zoo.

Our building, and all the others that bordered Central Park, now had vertical gardens running from the ground floor up to the roof, lush gardens with sunflowers and roses jutting out over the traffic lights.

People drifted by under a spell of wonder.

"First a cartwheel," Grandma said. "Now this."

A canopy of jungle vines hung over Fifth Avenue, tossed by trees inside the park onto street lamps on the other side the street.

"Central Park is part park, part jungle," Nikki said. "It's a pungle."

Bobby came running over. "Isn't it amazing?"

"Did we do this, Bobby?" I whispered so Grandma wouldn't hear.

"You're darn right we did."

We greedily inhaled an unfamiliar fragrance, a fresh forest scent not of this world.

Over by the boathouse, there grew a sycamore so colossal, no one dared to approach it. A poodle pulled free from its frightened master, pranced forward and peed on it. Everyone cheered. Dogs began to line up to relieve themselves on the towering sycamore. The word must've gotten out in the bird community. They were flying in from Connecticut to nest in its lofty branches.

Two dozen reporters stuck microphones in the face of a renowned scientist.

"How do you explain this?" one of them asked.

"I can't," said the scientist. "Don't ask me again."

He ran away with the reporters in hot pursuit.

The only person happier than us was the mayor.

"I'll definitely get reelected after this," he told his bodyguards.

We checked out YouTube on our smart phones. There were thousands of clips showing immaculate subways and sparkling skyscrapers on Wall Street, in Times Square. The entire island was green and pristine.

I met up with Tula behind a tree in Strawberry Fields.

"I got revenge on the princess," she said.

"Good," I said. "I hope she's dead."

"Worse than that. I planted a black butterfly inside her. Now she's in love with Stanley."

"No way," I said.

She popped open her briefcase. "See for yourself."

I peered inside the briefcase. Stanley and the princess were snuggling on a couch, taking turns spitting quarters across the room.

"You're the hottest parking meter I've ever seen," she said.

"I hear that from a lot of women," crooned the parking meter.

"You don't have a girlfriend, do you?"

"No, baby," said the parking meter. "I'm all yours."

She swooned. "You're my prince."

Tula closed her briefcase while I rolled around on the grass laughing. She directed my attention to a figure strolling across Strawberry Fields. "Someone wants to talk to you, Giles."

I rushed over to the judge. He was disguised as a construction worker in dirty overalls. It was definitely him. I don't know too many construction workers who sound like wind chimes when they walk.

"Your Honor!"

"That's right. It's me, Giles. I came here to inspect your city. And I must say, I'm very impressed. What impresses me the most is the manner in which you did it. It wasn't the technology and all the gadgets. Ultimately it came down to you kids. Thousands of children taking action, doing simple things. You have renewed our faith in your species. You children really do care. Congratulations, Giles. You have passed the test."

We shook hands. Dust particles floated in a figure eight around our clasped hands.

"It's the Pollendoozees," said the judge. "They came to join the celebration."

I waved Toshi and Almost Big Daddy to come on over. When I looked back at the judge, he was gone. So were the Pollendoozees.

Almost Big Daddy was depressed. I wrapped my arm around him.

"If I'm Big Daddy, then what I say goes. Is that right?" I said.

"Absolutely," the android murmured.

"Then I therefore issue a decree that from now on you are to be called Big Daddy."

His face brightened. "Are you sure?"

"I'm positive."

"What a relief. You have no idea how horrible it was being Almost Big Daddy." He got down on his hands and knees and kissed the ground. "Life is good. I'm Big Daddy again."

Toshi and the euphoric droid wandered off. They knew I wanted to be alone with Tula. I joined her behind the tree.

Both of us couldn't stop grinning.

"So are we going out on a date or what?" I said.

"Of course we are."

(Hey, reader, did you hear that? I'm finally going to kiss a girl!)

"I think I'll take you to the Regassa Nebulae," she said. "Their sunsets are amazing."

"When do we go?"

"I don't know. We'll figure it out. I'm due back in court right now and you have to go congratulate the other member of our team." She pointed at Navida on the other side of the field.

I whipped out the green vial. "I saved some star milk for Navida. In five minutes she'll be doing cartwheels too."

"No, she won't, Giles."

"Why not?"

"Giles, star milk is so concentrated, it will only work on those who have been drained of all life force. Navida has not been drained of life, Giles. Far from it. She's more alive than most of the people in this city. The star milk would explode inside her. Her system couldn't take it."

"Come on," I said. "Are you serious?"

"Heed my warning. What you hold in your hands could kill her."

"Then you do something, Tula. You can do anything."

"There's a limit to what I can do, Giles." Her blue face sank. "My father isn't well. There's nothing I can do for him either."

Tula wasn't a superhero. None of us were.

She gave me a hug and smiled. "Go say hi to your friend. She's looking for you."

Tula pressed the button on her briefcase and disappeared. I wandered over by Navida, who was marveling at the foliage. She beamed at her trees. "I'm the happiest girl on Earth."

The happiest girl on Earth couldn't be in a wheelchair, could she? Maybe she could. That thing on her face was too bright to be a smile. And yet that's what it was. The wind blew a piece of it onto my face. It was the same smile but on two faces. That's how big it was. It needed two faces to not feel all scrunched up.

"Come on," she said, "let's go check out the Sheep Meadow."

I pushed her along a winding path. We came upon a sunlit stream.

"I don't remember a stream being here," Navida said. "And look at that funny little bridge."

"Let's cross it," I said.

When we got to the other side, I glanced back over my shoulder. The Bridgeling winked at me.

I winked back.

I pushed my friend through the park.

It was one of those clear blue afternoons when the day belongs to the sky.

ACKNOWLEDGMENTS

I'd like to thank my agent, Rosemary Stimola, for the miracle of selling this book twenty-four hours after agreeing to represent me. My deepest gratitude to Liz Szabla and Kate Egan, for their exquisite editorial guidance. Thanks to Marlene Sway, for opening my eyes to the power of children's literature. Thanks to Eric Harabes, who has an uncanny knack for jump-starting my imagination. Thanks to Jared Cyr and Rick Adams, for the fuel of friendship. To Jim Miller, a tireless supporter of my writing. And special thanks to my girlfriend, Andrea, also known as Cozy Superstar.